MARLEE MATLIN

~

deaf child crossing

ALADDIN PAPERBACKS

New York London Toronto Sydney Singapore

First Aladdin Paperbacks edition March 2004

Copyright © 2002 by Marlee Matlin

ALADDIN PAPERBACKS
An imprint of Simon & Schuster
Children's Publishing Division
1230 Avenue of the Americas
New York, NY 10020

Also available in a Simon & Schuster Books for Young Readers hardcover edition.
Designed by O'Lanso Gabbidon
The text of this book was set in Bembo.
Manufactured in United States of America
10 9 8 7 6 5

The Library of Congress has cataloged the hardcover edition as follows:

Matlin, Marlee.
Deaf child crossing / Marlee Matlin.—1st ed.
p.cm.
Summary: Despite the fact that Megan is deaf and Cindy can hear, the two girls become friends when Cindy moves into Megan's neighborhood, but when they go away to camp, their friendship is put to the test.
ISBN-13: 978-0-689-82208-7 (hc.)
ISBN-10: 0-689-82208-1 (hc.)
[1. Best friends—Fiction. 2. Friendship—Fiction. 3. Deaf—Fiction. 4. People with disabilities—Fiction. 5. Camps—Fiction.] 1. Title
PZ7.M4312 De 2002
[Fic]—dc21
                                        2001057589

ISBN-13: 978-0-689-86696-8 (Aladdin pbk.)
ISBN-10: 0-689-86696-8 (Aladdin pbk.)

Cindy looked straight at Megan. Now she looked a little frustrated. "What's the matter? Are you deaf or something?" she yelled back.

Megan screamed out, and then fell to the ground, laughing hysterically. "How did you know that?" she asked as she laughed.

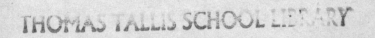

To my husband, Kevin, and my children, Sarah and Brandon, the constant light of my life. I love you.

~

There are a few people I'd like to thank. Without them this book could not have been possible. Firstly, to my dear friend, Lorna Luft, who encouraged me to tell this touching story, and who introduced me to the wonderful Alan Nevins in the Renaissance Division of AMG. My thanks also go out to David Gale and everyone at Simon & Schuster.

To my parents and family, I'd like to thank you for teaching me about self-esteem and allowing me to be independent. I couldn't have come this far without you. I'd also like to thank my original "BFF," Liz Tannebaum, who inspired a great deal of the story. And this book would not have been possible without the brilliant writing assistance of Rick Bitzelberger.

Finally, to my producing partner and my "left hand" man, Jack Jason, who helped put all the elements of this story together. Your input and ideas were invaluable. Thank you for all that you have done.

contents

~

are you deaf or something?

MEGAN SAT ON THE HOOD OF HER FATHER'S BIG
blue SUV, watching and waiting for a moving
truck to come rumbling down Morton Street
toward the Bregenzer house. *Of course,* Megan
thought, *it isn't really the Bregenzer house anymore. They moved out in April.* Practically every
day since the sign had come down, Megan had
asked her parents, "When are they moving in?"
And they always answered, "Pretty soon."
Megan knew they were teasing her, but that
didn't matter. The real estate agent who took
down the "For Sale" sign told the Merrills that
the new owners had a little girl nine years
old—the same age as Megan.

Hardly any kids Megan's age lived in her

neighborhood. And the ones who were her age were boys who lived two blocks over, and they weren't really her friends. So this new kid would be the first girl in the neighborhood in a long time. Megan had so many questions running through her head as she waited on the car hood and stared up at the puffy white clouds in the sky. What would the new kid be like? Would she be nice? Funny? What kind of toys would she bring with her? Megan hoped she would have new stuff, unlike the hand-me-down toys and too-big bike she got from her older brother, Matt. But, most of all, Megan wondered if the new girl would be like some of the kids at school who poked fun at her. Megan was tired of having to stick up for herself or have her brother yell at the kids who teased her. She scrunched up her eyes at the memory and pushed those thoughts out of her head. This girl would be different. She knew it. *Maybe,* Megan thought as she crossed her fingers for luck, *she'll be my best friend.*

It was the first Saturday of summer vacation, which meant no more homework and no more waking up at the crack of dawn to get to school. Megan scanned the street. Still no moving truck. She looked down at all the huge oak and maple trees on Morton Street, all perfectly lined up on each side of the block. She always wondered if they grew that way or if someone had planted the little saplings in perfect straight lines with rulers when they'd built the street. They were beautiful, towering trees, with big trunks perfect for hiding around during hide-and-seek and low limbs just right for climbing on.

Sometimes on dark winter nights, when the trees had no leaves, Megan imagined the trees turning into giant walking sticks, like the kind she saw in the traveling bug zoo at school. But instead of swallowing unsuspecting flies and spiders, these giant walking sticks swallowed up people and their pets as they walked by. At least that's what Megan's brother, Matt, told her when Mrs. Adams's fat tabby cat turned up missing.

"Probably got eaten up by the trees," Matt said. Megan didn't believe him then, but one night, during a real scary thunderstorm, when some tree branches scraped against their house, Megan was convinced that the trees were coming for them! Her mother told her she was being silly; "trees can't come alive and snatch people." Megan wasn't completely convinced. And just in case, she showed the trees her respect and never carved words on them or peeled off their bark like other kids did.

Megan's nose tickled; it was the smell of freshly cut grass, the perfect summer smell. Megan rolled over on her side and saw old Mr. Rogowski mowing his lawn. Every weekend, unless it was raining, old Mr. Rogowski was out mowing his lawn. Megan's dad made Matt mow the lawn for his allowance, but he always grumbled. Mr. Rogowski never seemed happier than when he was cutting his grass. He was a short little man with a bald spot on the back of his head and had only three fingers on his left hand, which made the kids who lived on the next block over afraid of him. But Mr. Rogowski was always nice to

Megan, and besides, Megan's father told her that there was nothing to be afraid of. Mr. Rogowski had lost his fingers in a lawn mower accident, and he was still happy cutting the grass. Megan smiled at the big floppy hat he wore to keep the sun off his bald spot; it was exactly like the hat her mother wore when they went to the beach. Mr. Rogowski looked up from his mower and waved at Megan. She waved back. Megan made it her business to know every person and pet in the neighborhood. Why not? It was Megan's street, and everyone in the neighborhood knew that.

Just then Megan looked up and saw a big truck coming to a stop at the driveway of the Bregenzer home. *The movers came up the other end of Morton Street! That was sneaky*, Megan thought, laughing to herself. She jumped down from the hood of the car and ran across the street to see her new neighbors.

Megan scurried up to the big oak that was right next to the driveway. From here she could peek around the trunk and watch all the action. Her first look was disappointing. She only saw three moving men starting to work at the back of the truck. They were all wearing gray coveralls with the sleeves cut off and red bandannas tied around their foreheads. Megan noticed their arm muscles because Matt was trying hard to grow his. Megan was going to tell Matt that he should become a mover if he wanted his muscles to grow really big.

But where were the new neighbors? The movers began to unload boxes. And more boxes, and more boxes and more boxes! Megan made sure she saw everything. She looked at the furniture and even the brand-new gardening tools. To Megan, personal belongings said a lot about their owners.

Megan paid close attention to the living room furniture that the movers were bringing in; a long sofa to lie on that she later found out was called a chaise, and two end tables made of dark wood with gleaming handles. How could someone sit in that furniture and watch television? It seemed so stiff and straight!

And then a car pulled up, right behind the moving van. At first it was hard for Megan to see because the June sun was reflecting brightly off of the window, and she had to cover her eyes. But then the doors swung open, and out stepped a couple. The man was tall and thin, with black hair combed very neatly and glasses that he kept pushing back up his nose. The woman was very pretty, with black curly hair just as neat as the man's hair. They both wore pressed tan pants and crisp white shirts. *Very clean for moving,* Megan thought.

So where is their daughter? she wondered. They're supposed to have a daughter! She remembered the Hammers who lived down the street who had no kids. Mr. Hammer was always chasing kids off his lawn when they tried to play in his leaf piles. Once he had even gone so far as to turn the hose on them. Megan thought it was because he had no kids and didn't understand that sometimes kids just need to jump in leaf piles; she hoped this new couple moving in wouldn't be the same. She crossed her fingers again and ventured closer to the car.

Megan now noticed that the man shouted something over to his wife as he walked up to the new house, but Megan had no idea what he was saying. Megan could tell by their anxious looks that moving day was very stressful for them. Suddenly, another bright reflection from a window flashed in Megan's face, and then she saw the rear of the station wagon open up.

Out stepped a little girl.

The first thing Megan noticed was that she had big brown eyes. Bigger and more brown than even Nancy Culver's, who sat behind Megan in her homeroom class and who had the biggest eyes Megan had ever seen. Nancy liked to gross out the kids in the class by turning her eyelids inside out. The next thing Megan noticed was the new girl's black hair. It was short and wavy, with tight little curls in the back, just like the girl's mother standing next to the car. Megan thought the hairstyle looked a little old-fashioned.

But Megan was still thrilled that the girl was really here. She ran over right to the car.

"Hi there!" yelled Megan, and the young girl nearly jumped out of her sandals. "I'm Megan" she continued to yell, "and I live four houses down from you! I think we should be new best friends!"

. Megan knew that her voice sounded different to others, since she couldn't tell how loud or soft she was speaking. Some people said it sounded like she was talking in a box, while others said it sounded like she was imitating a cartoon voice. Still, once people had time to get used to Megan's special way of talking, they didn't seem to have any trouble understanding her.

Megan watched as the girl with the big brown eyes opened them so wide that it almost looked to Megan as if she weren't blinking at all. For a second, Megan imagined that old cartoon where the wolf's eyes pop out and his jaw drops to the ground. This made Megan grin a little. Although she had been speaking this way since she had started taking speech classes at age three, no one had ever been *this* surprised to hear her voice.

"Hi," said the little girl finally. She shyly tucked her chin to her shoulder when she talked.

"Hi!" Megan repeated with the same voice. "My name is Megan. What's yours?"

The little girl seemed to understand her better this time. "Cindy," she responded quietly, still looking down at the grass. "Cindy Calicchio."

"What?" asked Megan. She couldn't hear her and fiddled with her hearing aids.

"Cindy," said the little girl in a louder voice, but she still didn't look up from the grass.

"I still don't understand you!" Megan yelled. Cindy's mom turned to see why the two girls were yelling at each other.

Cindy looked straight at Megan. Now *she* looked a little frustrated. "What's the matter? Are you *deaf* or something?" she yelled back.

Megan screamed out and then fell to the ground, laughing hysterically. "How did you know that?" she asked as she laughed.

"Huh? You mean you *are* deaf?" Cindy asked meekly.

"Duh! That's why I have these hearing aids!" Megan said as she pointed to her ears and turned her head from side to side so that Cindy could see the bright purple ear molds and hearing aids hanging over each ear. "I am deaf."

Cindy took a moment to let this sink in. "I thought someone put bubble gum in your ears!" she said.

Megan laughed even harder at the thought.

Cindy waited for Megan to stop laughing before she tried asking her another question. "What do they do?" she asked timidly.

"They make everything loud for me. Even though I can't hear a lot of things, I can hear some things with these," said Megan as she stood up again. She purposely turned the little dial on one of the hearing aids until it made a loud squeaking sound like a teakettle that was boiling over. "They're like the headphones my dad wears when he doesn't want my mom to hear his goofy music. Except, for me, they make *sounds*, not just music, louder."

"You mean you can hear? But I thought you were deaf . . . ," said Cindy.

Megan could see that Cindy was very confused. She went on, anyway. "I can hear a little, but with these on, I can hear more! It's not as much as you can hear, but it helps. And they'll help even more if you look at me when you talk."

Cindy's cheeks flushed with embarrassment.

"Can I finish my lecture now?" Megan asked as she put her hands on her hips.

Cindy giggled and nodded, looking more relaxed. More than that, she looked like she understood everything Megan was saying.

"So you're Megan, right?" asked Cindy cautiously.

Megan nodded enthusiastically. She knew Cindy wasn't confused anymore, and that was the most important thing to her. "Hi, Cindy!" she said, beaming her biggest smile. "Welcome to my neighborhood."

Megan grabbed Cindy's hand and shook it

hard. Cindy looked surprised by Megan's grip, but after a moment she shook it right back.

"It's going to be an awesome summer," said Megan.

CHAPTER 2

~

apples, sit!

THE NEXT MORNING, CINDY WOKE UP TO FIND
her mother standing over her bed with a letter
in her hand. "Looks like you win the prize for
getting the first piece of mail in the new
house," said Grace.

Cindy rubbed her eyes, adjusting to the
bright sunlight pouring in from the windows.
"I suppose we'll have to hang up your curtains
today," Grace said. Cindy wasn't really paying
attention; she was too curious about her letter.

The envelope was bright purple and had
dark green frog stickers on the left side. There
was no postmark and no return address, but it
was definitely addressed to her. "Who would

write a letter so quickly?" she wondered out loud. She opened the envelope and found a printed invitation inside:

CINDY
YOU ARE INVITED TO THE HOME OF
MEGAN
9509 MORTON STREET
THIS MORNING AT 10:00 SHARP!

Cindy couldn't believe her eyes. She had never gotten anything like this in her life! She looked at her clock and sat up in shock—it was already 9:45! She usually got up at 7:30, but she had forgotten to set her alarm clock and her mom must have let her sleep in. Cindy wasn't sure what she should do.

Her mother peeked over her shoulder to read the purple page.

"Looks like you also win the prize for making the first friend in the neighborhood," she said.

"I guess so." Cindy shrugged.

"Then you'd better hurry up and get dressed."

"But what about my stuff?" Cindy asked. Her room was full of boxes that needed unpacking. And that was nothing compared to all the boxes in the rest of the house.

"I suppose your father and I can spare you for a few hours," said Grace. "Besides, it's rude to be late for an invitation," she added as she left the room.

Cindy looked around her new bedroom. She didn't like the idea of all her things still stuffed away in those boxes. Cindy liked to have everything in order. All her clothes and toys and dolls and books . . . they all had a special place. But on the other hand, she was very curious about this Megan girl. Cindy made up her mind. She threw on her shorts and sandals and T-shirt and hurried downstairs. She ran outside without even eating her cereal.

But when she got to the address on her invitation, Cindy slowed down. She began to pace up and down the sidewalk in front of Megan's house, feeling very anxious. She wasn't very good at making new friends. Sometimes Cindy wished she had a little sister or brother. At least that way she'd always have a built-in friend and wouldn't have to worry about making new ones.

Back in the city where she'd lived before, Cindy had been by herself most of the time. The other kids who lived on her block tended to ignore her, so she spent her time playing quietly in her room or reading at the library. She loved to read and was always checking out armloads of books. But now she was the new girl in a new neighborhood. This was a big deal for her.

Megan's house was pretty much like all the other houses on Morton Street. It was painted dark brown and had white lacy curtains in the windows. There were colorful flowers on the front porch in little planters, and a hedge that ran all around the driveway. *It was a friendly house. It didn't look like a deaf girl lived there,* she thought.

Cindy took a deep breath and walked up the path to the house. The front door was open, but the screen door was closed. She could hear the sound of loud rock music playing. Cindy rang the doorbell but was afraid no one would hear. She rang again. This time, she smashed her face against the screen door for a peek and saw what looked like a fireworks display. Lights were flashing all over the house. Cindy wondered if she had broken something by ringing the doorbell.

"Hello?" Cindy called through the door as best she could without sounding rude. Suddenly, a woman appeared. Cindy almost let out a little scream, she was so startled.

"You must be Megan's friend, Cindy. I'm Lainee, Megan's mother."

"Nice to meet you," said Cindy. She liked Megan's mom right away. Lainee opened the door to let Cindy step inside. To Cindy, Lainee looked like an adult version of Megan, with her quick smile and large blue eyes. But Lainee spoke with a firm voice that was different from Megan's. Cindy looked at Lainee's ears. She wasn't wearing any hearing aids. She was confused.

"Is something wrong?" Lainee asked.

"You don't have those bubble gum hearing

aids in your ears like Megan," Cindy blurted out.

"Bubble gum? Good heavens, what are you talking about?" Lainee asked.

Now Cindy was embarrassed. She looked down and shuffled her feet. "Megan showed me her hearing aids. I thought they looked like wads of purple bubble gum. How come you don't have them?" Cindy hoped she was making some kind of sense to Megan's mother.

Lainee laughed, not as hard as Megan had yesterday, but Cindy could tell it was the same sort of laugh.

"I can hear just like you," Lainee said, "so I don't need to wear hearing aids. Megan wasn't born deaf, either, but she got very sick when she was a baby, and when her fever finally came down she had lost most of her hearing." Lainee pointed upstairs, past the living room "Why don't you go upstairs and find Megan? She's in her room."

On the way up the stairs, Cindy noticed the living room furniture. There was an overstuffed couch and several chairs that looked like they had seen better days. There was a huge television set that was on, but the sound was turned off. This was completely different from Cindy's house; her parents wouldn't allow their television in the living room. At Cindy's house, the living room was for company only, and the television was in the den.

Cindy wouldn't have noticed anything more about the TV set except that there were little black lines with words popping up on the screen. Cindy would have to ask Megan about that. At the top of the stairs, Cindy wasn't sure which room to go into until she heard the sound of Megan's voice.

"Apples, sit . . . Apples sit!"

Cindy had figured Megan was different from other girls she had met, but talking to fruit—that was *really* crazy. Maybe it would be better to come back another time."

Apples, I said sit!" Megan said loudly. Cindy decided she was too curious to go home and she wanted to see who Megan was talking to. She walked toward the room where she heard Megan.

"Apples! When are you ever going to listen to me?" Megan scolded as Cindy peeked around the corner.

To Cindy's surprise, Megan was talking and moving her hands to a dog. Suddenly Megan looked up.

"Hi, Cindy! You're right on time!" Megan said as she pointed to the clock on the wall. It was the biggest clock that Cindy had ever seen, and she noticed that Megan grinned even bigger than the day before, when they had first met.

Wow, this is really different, thought Cindy as she looked around the room. Even though there were the usual posters of movie stars like Freddie Prinze, Jr., and Heath Ledger, the rest of the room was like something out of a Dr. Seuss book. First of all, everything was purple.

On the wood floor was a purple rug with butterflies on it. The bed, which was like the bed Cindy's mom had in her sewing room and which she called a daybed, had a purple bedspread with big purple pillows. Even the trundle bed underneath, the kind you could pull out when friends or company came by to spend the night, had a purple bedspread on it.

Next to the bed was a big purple beanbag chair. It was thrown up against a wall that was purple, though the wall wasn't quite the same shade as everything else. Megan even had Rollerblades and a computer that were purple!

And books lined the shelves everywhere. Cindy recognized some of the same Judy Blume titles that she had read. Megan even had Tamagotchi, little Japanese cyber toys, and Dreamsicles, collectible angel figurines, lining the shelves. And Megan certainly couldn't be called neat. There were clothes thrown everywhere. There was even a sock dangling from the ceiling fan! On the floor by Megan's bed were scraps of purple paper, scissors, and a roll of frog stickers. This must be where Megan had made the invitation.

Between the blaring music and this wild room, Cindy was in a purple fog. She put her hands over her ears. "Why is your music so LOUD?" she asked.

Megan roared with laughter. "Because, silly, I'm deaf!"

Megan walked over to her boom box and turned down the volume just enough so Cindy didn't have to cover her ears.

"This is Apples," Megan said. "He's thirteen years old and doesn't listen to anything I say."

Cindy looked down at Apples. He was a strange-looking dog, with a face full of chin whiskers like an old man. Cindy noticed that his eyes were milky white where the dark part of the eyeball should be, and his mouth had no teeth in it. Still, at least he wasn't purple!

"Apples? Why did you pick that name?" Cindy asked.

"Once, way before I was born, my family went to the country to pick apples and right under the sign that said 'Apple Picking' was another sign that said 'Puppies for Free.' One puppy ran right up to my brother, Matt, and jumped up and down on his leg. Matt picked up the puppy, called him Apples, and we've had him ever since."

"Oh . . . ," said Cindy, distracted by the purple curtains that hung by the window. She was really grateful for her white room.

"The only bad thing about Apples," Megan said as she scrunched up her face, "is being that he's so old, he has no teeth, he can't see very well, and has the grossest breath you have ever smelled!"

Apples looked up at Megan and wagged his tail. Cindy wondered if the dog knew they were talking about him.

"No treats now, Apples!" said Megan. Cindy watched again as Megan talked to Apples with her voice and her hands.

"What are you doing?" asked Cindy.

"I'm using sign language with Apples, but he only listens to Matt," Megan explained.

Megan continued to move her hands in a flurry as she said, "But Apples knows that I sneak him treats if he begs. That's why he always follows me."

Cindy moved over to the bed and sat down. "Who's that singing?" asked Cindy as she scrunched up her nose. It reminded Cindy of the stuff her dad liked to listen to in the car. Old people's music.

"It's Billy Joel." Megan smiled as she closed the bedroom door to reveal a huge poster of a man with dark sunglasses on. "Isn't he cool?"

"Who is Billy Joel?" Cindy asked. She had never heard of him.

"That's what all my friends ask me," Megan replied. "My parents love him. He's a rock singer from a million years ago. I think it was the eighties or something. I like his music because his words are easy for me to follow."

Cindy was feeling confused all over again. Maybe it was too much purple. Maybe it was the idea of a dog with no teeth with bad breath and bad eyesight. Or maybe it was because Cindy just couldn't understand how a girl who couldn't hear could follow the words to a song.

Megan motioned to Cindy to get her attention. "Watch me," Megan said as she pushed a button on the boom box and selected a track from the CD player. Then she pulled out a sheet of music and put it on Cindy's lap. The music began. Megan pointed to the words for Cindy as Billy Joel sang:

Don't go changing, to try and please me
You never let me down before
Don't imagine you're too familiar
And I don't see you anymore . . .

Cindy couldn't believe that every time the words played on the stereo, Megan pointed to the right words.

"That is so neat!" Cindy said as Megan proudly pointed to more words along with the music. "How did you do that?"

Megan leaned over to the stereo and paused the music. "My father bought me the sheet music with all the words," said Megan. "I listened with my hearing aid turned way up until I knew what sound matched what word. Simple, huh? And now that I know the words, I also sign the song," Megan said proudly.

"Sing?" said Cindy. Cindy wondered what a girl who couldn't hear would sound like if she sang. Cindy remembered that her mother, who sang in a church choir back at their old home, was always complaining about Mrs.

Woodman. Mrs. Woodman was tone-deaf, and she couldn't sing even if every angel in heaven came down and showed her how, said her mother. Cindy wondered if that's what it sounded like when Megan sang.

Megan looked at Cindy's scrunched-up face. "Not sing . . . SIGN! You know, move my hands?"

Cindy was lost.

"Promise you won't make fun?" asked Megan.

"I promise," Cindy said, even though she wasn't sure what Megan meant about signing a song.

Megan got up from the daybed and pressed another button. The song began as Megan closed her eyes. Suddenly as the music played, Megan began to sway to the music! Cindy was mesmerized. Megan moved to the rhythm as if she could *hear!* Cindy couldn't believe it. Then the words began to play:

> *Don't go changing, to try and please me*
> *You never let me down before . . .*

Right on cue, as if someone were telling Megan what to do, Megan began to move her hands along with Billy Joel's voice. Her hands seemed to float in the air like butterflies, each butterfly representing a word. It almost looked as if her hands were in control of the music. Even Megan's face and body moved in perfect unison to the music. For a moment, Cindy actually thought she could understand what Megan was saying, without speaking. For Cindy, Megan's face and hand movements seemed to make sense to her. She had never seen anything as beautiful in her life. Finally, Billy Joel sang:

I could not love you any better
I love you just the way you are.

When the song was over, Megan closed her hands and bowed her head like a ballerina after a dance. Cindy applauded and whistled so loud that even Megan noticed and looked up. Cindy was smiling from ear to ear.

"That was the most fantastic, awesome, and stupendous thing I have ever seen," Cindy said. "How did you learn how to do that?"

"I had Matt go over the song with me until I had every word and every beat memorized," said Megan.

"Wow!" said Cindy. "He must really like the song to teach it to you."

Megan let out a snort. "He hates the song! I play it every day, at least twenty times—really loud. It drives him bonkers!"

Suddenly, Lainee appeared at the doorway. Cindy noticed that she talked with her hands when she spoke to Megan.

"Megan, you're going to have to turn your music down. It's your brother's turn to listen to his music," she said.

"Tell him to get hearing aids!" Megan responded. She looked over at Cindy and crossed her eyes. Cindy had to clamp her hand over her mouth to stop from laughing out loud.

"Turn the music down now," said Lainee sternly. Cindy recognized that tone in Mrs. Merrill's voice. She had heard it a million times from her own mother. Megan turned the music down.

"Boy, you're lucky you can't hear some-times," said Cindy. "My mom yells at me like that when I don't pay attention."

"Yeah," said Megan. "But I looked at her face, and for me, it's the same thing as hearing her. Didn't you see all those veins pop out of the sides of her neck? When that happens, I know she means business. Parents can be such a pain sometimes." Cindy never talked that way about her parents, although her parents could be a pain, too, sometimes.

Cindy was getting used to the purple room now. She looked down at Apples, who was sitting on the floor next to Megan.

"What do you do if you can't go outside or your mom won't let you play your music?" Cindy asked as she leaned down to pet Apples. Cindy suddenly noticed that Megan was right: Apples did have bad breath.

"You ask a lot of questions!" Megan said, laughing. And with that, she turned around and flicked on her computer.

"Here's my rainy-day-can't-play-music-can't-watch-too-much-TV answer!" said Megan

with a flourish. And with that, the computer
screen lit up, and the words "Megan's Room"
appeared. In purple, of course. Cindy laughed.
She realized that with Megan, anything goes.

Megan began typing on her computer and,
quicker than she could blink, Megan was surfing
the Internet. Cindy couldn't believe how fast
Megan could type without even looking at the
keys. Cindy always had to hunt for each letter, so
it took her forever to finish a single sentence.

"Welcome!" said the computer. The words
flashed on the screen at the same time. Cindy
sat watching Megan's fingers tap out words on
the keyboard.

"What is this?" asked Cindy.

"It's called the Playground," said Megan.

Cindy watched as Megan's name popped
up on the screen under the title "My
Playground." Suddenly, other names began
popping up on the screen. "Madeleine,"
"Zack," and "Sarah."

"Who are all those people?" asked Cindy.

"They're all my cyber friends," replied
Megan.

Cindy had surfed the Net at the library but had never gone into a chat room. She was never sure what to say. Maybe she would get her own computer for her next birthday and be able to learn to type as fast as Megan. She stared at Megan's computer as everyone signed on to the Playground and started typing like crazy.

"Hi, Megan! It's Zack."

"Where have you been?" typed Madeleine. "I've been waiting to say hi for the last half hour!"

"She's probably listening to her oldies music again," typed Sarah.

Megan typed out her response: "Be nice."

"Awesome!" said Cindy.

Megan kept on typing and laughing with her friends on the computer. "Are they all deaf like you?" Cindy asked.

"I don't know," Megan said, like she'd never really thought about it. "Maybe they are but maybe they're not. It doesn't make a difference here." She turned around in her chair. "Pretty cool, huh? Want to try it?"

"I don't know," said Cindy. What if she typed the wrong thing?

"Don't worry," said Megan. "But let me introduce you first." Megan typed fast and furiously on the keyboard.

"Hi, everybody. I want to introduce you to Cindy. She's my new neighbor," typed Megan. "She's also my new best friend . . ."

Cindy couldn't believe Megan had said that. She never had a best friend before in her life.

Cindy slowly typed "hi." Everyone typed back a greeting. It was too fast for Cindy.

"You'd better take over," she told Megan. Megan put the keyboard on her lap and began typing away. *So this is my new best friend,* Cindy thought, and smiled. She looked over at Megan, who was smiling just as big.

CHAPTER 3

~

telephones are stupid

"TELEPHONES ARE STUPID. EVERYONE IS ALWAYS on the phone, phone, phone!" said Megan as she stomped around her living room. "Why is it so important that you have to talk on the phone all the time?"

Megan was bored. It was the Monday after Cindy had moved in, and Cindy had to go off and spend the day shopping with her mother. So now Megan had no one to play with. She went outside and played with Apples for a while, but Apples didn't want to play, so she decided to come back in the house and talk to her mother. Megan called for her mother, but she didn't answer. She tried calling out again.

Then her mom popped her head out of the doorway, holding the phone receiver.

"I'm on the phone, honey. Before you start screaming at the top of your lungs, you need to check around the house. It's the polite thing to do," Lainee said.

Her mother was right. But Megan was still frustrated that her mother was doing something that she couldn't do very well—talk on the phone. But instead of saying "I know" or "I'm sorry," it came out as, "Telephones are stupid! Everyone is always on the phone, phone, phone!"

"I don't recall stomping around your room when you're on the computer chatting with your friends," said Lainee. "Speaking of your room, if you're really bored you might try cleaning up that disaster area." That was Mom's answer for everything. "Why don't you clean up your room?"

"I have a better idea," Megan said. "Let's bake a chocolate cake with gooey frosting." But before her mom could answer, she held up a finger to Megan and started talking on the phone again.

Megan went back to the living room and flopped down on the sofa. She clicked on the television remote and flipped past a couple of channels. But nothing held her interest. This whole telephone business was frustrating.

Mom, Dad, and Matt were always talking and talking into that silly plastic mouthpiece. Every time they talked they would make faces. They would pause, laugh, and then pause again. What could possibly be so interesting? And Matt would never tell her who he was talking with. He must have girlfriends, because sometimes he would blush or turn away when she tried to read his lips while he was on the phone.

"Mom, who are you talking to, anyway?" Megan yelled out from the living room.

Lainee poked her head inside the room with the phone still pressed to her ear. Then she signed without using her voice, "It's Grandma Josie!"

"Grandma Josie! I want to say hello!" Megan exclaimed. She jumped up from the sofa and ran to her mother, forgetting all about her frustration with the phone. Her mother handed her the receiver.

"HI, GRANDMA!" Megan shouted into the phone. Lainee gently pulled the receiver away from Megan's mouth and explained for the umpteenth time that she didn't need to shout into the phone.

Megan lowered her voice, "Grandma, it's me, Megan! I didn't mean to shout. Did I scare you?" Lainee leaned down to listen in. Megan was more than happy to share the phone.

"Grandma Josie is laughing. She says you didn't scare her and she's happy to hear your voice," Lainee signed to Megan. "She said she's waiting for your next letter. It's your turn to write."

Megan nodded her head. She loved writing to Grandma Josie. And she loved it when Grandma Josie wrote back. Her grandmother's letters were beautifully written, like the letters on the penmanship chart at school. All perfect loops and straight lines. In one letter, Grandma Josie called Megan her favorite grandchild. She made sure Matt saw that letter. And even when Matt told her that Grandma Josie called all her grandchildren her favorites, it didn't matter. Grandma Josie was *her* favorite Grandma.

Of all the letters that Grandma Josie sent Megan, the one she remembered the most was the one that was attached to a big box. The whole family had gathered around and waited for her to open it up. Inside were all these squiggly things. Her father called them "packing peanuts." What kind of silly present is this? But when she dug, she found the real present—a pink velvet box. She remembered Matt waving his hands in the air. "Girl stuff."

Megan had looked up at her mother, who was smiling the kind of smile she had seen before. It was the "Isn't that nice?" smile. But usually the "Isn't that nice?" smile meant that whatever mom was smiling at wasn't nice at all. How could she smile like that with such a beautiful little box?

But when Megan opened up the box, it suddenly didn't matter what her mother was thinking. Inside the box was a tiny delicate ballerina, dressed in pink, doing her pirouettes in front of a small mirror. It was beautiful. The ballerina turned round and round, and Megan pictured herself as the dancer, spinning across the stage. It was the best gift that Grandma had ever sent.

"Tell Grandma I'll call her again soon," Megan told Lainee with a smile. She handed back the phone.

Lainee laughed. "Now, that's very good phone manners, Megan."

"See? I can use the phone just as good as anybody," Megan said in response.

When she was through with her phone call, Lainee went off to the store, and Megan spent some time chatting with her cyber friends. Later that afternoon, the house was empty except for Megan. Matt was outside mowing the lawn. Mom was out shopping with her friends. And Megan's dad was at work. Megan kept thinking about the phone. It wasn't fair that everyone else could talk on the phone and she couldn't.

Megan turned on her TDD, which was short for Telecommunications Device for the Deaf. It was a small device that looked like a little white typewriter that was connected to the phone. With someone else on the other end with a TDD, she could type back and forth and letters would scroll by on a little screen, sort of like a portable Internet chat room for just two people.

But it wasn't the same as *talking on the phone*. She wanted to do what *everyone* could do. Megan's dad had once told her she had a stubborn streak. She remembered she had run upstairs and looked in the mirror but hadn't seen any streak on her back. But that didn't matter. If everyone was playing outside, she wanted to play outside. If everyone was watching TV, she wanted to watch TV. She didn't want to be the only one left out just because she couldn't hear.

Megan remembered what her mother said about her "good phone manners." Why not put those manners to good use now? She decided to make her first phone call, without a TDD. On the hearing aid that hung behind her ear, she switched a little button to "T," which meant "telephone." It was the button that made things louder on the telephone. Then she lifted the phone to her ear. She could hear *something*! It was a steady hum.

But what was Grandma Josie's telephone number? She remembered her mother pushing the Operator button sometimes when she had a question. So she did the same thing.

After a few seconds, Megan "heard" a voice. But what it was saying? At least that humming had stopped.

"Hello? I'm Megan and I want to talk to Mrs. Josie Merrill," said Megan into the telephone. But all she heard was a bunch of far-away sounds that didn't seem to have a beginning or an end. The most Megan could hear was "mrttrssttbbffnmtthhur."

It was frustrating. Then she remembered about the other buttons on the phone, buttons that had names next to them. Her mother called them "speed dial." Megan liked that. It was like the telephone became a race car, speeding around the track waiting for someone to answer it. Sometimes she saw mom or dad just press one of those speed dial buttons and in a second they were talking to someone. Sure enough, there was Grandma Josie's name next to a button.

Megan lifted the phone to her hearing aid and pushed the button that said "Grandma Josie." Suddenly the low humming sound she had heard when she picked up the phone stopped. Then she heard more sounds, but they were like spaced-apart beeps and pauses. Then they stopped, and she heard a sound that seemed like someone was talking.

"Grandma Josie?" shouted Megan, and then she remembered her phone manners. "Grandma?" said Megan more softly.

There was no other sound. No hums, beeps, or talking. What happened? Maybe the speed dial got a flat tire. She hung up the phone, waited for five seconds, then picked up the receiver and pushed the button again . . . and again . . . and again.

Just then, Lainee walked into the room with

an armload of grocery bags. "What are you doing?" she asked as she gently put down her grocery bags on the dining room table.

Megan felt like she wanted to cry. "I'm trying to call Grandma Josie, but the phone is broke!"

Her mother listened to the receiver. She spoke a few words and listened. Finally she hung up. "Did you really call Grandma Josie ten times?" asked Lainee.

Megan couldn't hold back any longer. Tears streamed down her face. "It's not fair! I want to use the phone like you and Daddy and Matt!" she shouted. She tried her best not to cry anymore, but she couldn't help it. She buried her head in her mother's arms.

Her mother let Megan cry for a moment. Then she lifted her face to wipe off her tears. "You know, sometimes there are things we just can't do."

Megan didn't understand.

"Like when Daddy wants to beat Matt in basketball, or Matt tries a somersault dive in the pool."

"Belly flop," Megan said, and she smiled a little.

"But there are ways that we all make up for it," Lainee told her.

"Like what?" Megan asked as she sniffled.

Lainee took out a tissue from her pocket, held it to Megan's nose, and Megan blew. Then Lainee lifted Megan's chin and looked right into her eyes. "You have a beautiful face, an intelligent and curious mind, and a marvelous personality. What more could you ask for?" Lainee asked.

"To use the phone like you," Megan replied. Lainee sighed and pushed Megan's bangs off her forehead.

"Well, for some things, you need a little help," Lainee said, trying to comfort her.

"But that's just it," Megan said, "I don't want help!" She stomped out of the kitchen, and this time her mother didn't stop her.

~

what's the sign for . . . ?

THAT AFTERNOON WHILE CINDY WAS OUT grocery shopping with her mom, her mind was still whirling over all the new things she had experienced at Megan's house the day before. Flashing lights, a funny little dog who had bad breath and who was blind, a room where everything was purple, and "singing" to music with your hands. It was all so amazing.

"Your head has been in the clouds today," said her mother.

"Huh?" was all Cindy managed to say.

"That's what I'm talking about," her mother said, smiling. "We even went right past the cereal aisle without you picking out your favorite."

"We did?" Cindy couldn't believe she had missed that.

"What's been on your mind?"

Cindy was happy to tell her mother all about Megan. She went on and on about her purple room and Apples and playing the music really loud. By the time she finished, they were past the checkout and pushing their shopping cart through the parking lot.

"So are you going to learn how to talk with your new friend?" asked Grace as she loaded up the groceries in the trunk of their car.

What did she mean? So far, there was no problem talking with Megan. "Megan understands me when I look at her and talk loudly," said Cindy.

"Megan probably has to read your lips, Cindy. It's not fair to have her do all the work talking with you. Maybe you could learn sign language," said Grace. "You know, start with the ABCs?"

She hadn't thought about that, but it made perfect sense. They were both in the car now, buckling up their seat belts.

"How would I learn that?" Cindy asked excitedly.

"Well, you can start with a trip to the library," Grace answered.

"Now?"

"I suppose," Grace said as she started the car.

The library was on the way home. It was Cindy's first time there, and the minute she walked through the big oak doors she felt right at home. While her mother signed them up for library cards, Cindy couldn't believe the rows and rows of books. There was even an upstairs! It was much bigger than her old library. At her old library Cindy had liked to challenge herself to see how fast she could find a book. She had gotten pretty good at knowing where everything was, from archeology to zoology. She couldn't wait to explore this place, but right now she was on a mission.

Cindy found the computer index and typed in "sign language." Sure enough there were several books on the subject. She jotted down the book number and went off in search of the right aisle. In no time she had found the right aisle. Of course she needed to use the little step-on wheels to reach up to the shelf she needed. And there she found the book she was looking for: *How to Speak with Your Hands.*

Cindy checked out the book. On the way home she marveled at all the pictures and descriptions of the many words in sign language. At the beginning of the book was the finger-spelling alphabet with a different hand position for each letter. It seemed so complicated. Cindy turned to her mother. "How could anyone learn all this?"

"Oh, it's easy," Grace said, and with that she began finger spelling the alphabet. Cindy couldn't believe her eyes!

"A, B, C, D . . . ," said Cindy's mother as she used a different hand shape for each letter until she reached the letter "Z."

Cindy followed along in her book. "Mom! You never told me you knew sign language!" Cindy exclaimed.

"Well, I don't know the whole language. Only how to finger spell the alphabet," said

Grace. "I learned when I was a Girl Scout. I guess it stuck with me."

When they finally pulled into the driveway, Cindy jumped out of the car and hurried to help Grace bring in the groceries. Once inside the kitchen, Cindy quickly helped put the food away as fast as she could.

"Slow down," her mother called after her. "You might break the eggs."

Grace began to make some lunch for both of them—tuna salad with lots of pickles and no onions, Cindy's favorite. But Cindy wanted to learn to sign. She pulled up a chair and waited. Her mother smiled down at her.

"Okay, but I'm a little rusty," she said as she formed the first letter "A" and motioned for Cindy to follow along. Cindy followed her mother as she spelled each letter of the alphabet. Before she knew it, she was at "Z."

"You remembered all of the letters!" said Cindy. She could see that her mother was very proud of herself.

"And you followed along perfectly!" said Grace.

"Let's practice all day, then I can surprise Megan by memorizing the whole alphabet!" Cindy said.

And that's just what they did. Both Cindy and her mother practiced so much that they got cramps in their hands. Sometimes Cindy had to ask for help with the proper placement of her fingers and thumbs, but it was turning out not to be so complicated after all. They practiced all day and even into the night. The last thing Cindy did before she fell asleep was spell out the alphabet on her fingers and she didn't pause once.

The next morning over breakfast, Cindy and her mom were finger spelling every word, every conversation to each other.

"Are you two planning a surprise birthday party?" asked Cindy's dad, Jack, from behind his newspaper. "You know I don't like surprises. In fact, its not even my birthday!"

It was the first time she had ever heard her father speak while he was reading his newspaper. Usually, he just sat there quietly and sipped his coffee and ate his breakfast. He never said a word; that's how much he liked reading the paper in the morning.

"We're just talking with each other, Daddy." Cindy giggled.

"Well, don't be so loud . . . ," he said as he peeked out from behind his paper.

"Oh, Daddy!" said Cindy. He was just joking.

Cindy spelled to her mother, "C-A-N I G-O T-O M-M-M—" Cindy got another cramp. Sign language definitely needs strong hands.

"Megan's?" asked her mother. "Go right ahead. Have fun!"

Cindy raced over to Megan's house and pressed the doorbell. Then she pressed her face against the screen door again to see the flashing lights. None of this was strange today! She could barely contain her excitement. She was going to surprise her new best friend! But nobody was answering the door.

All at once, a cute boy appeared at the screen door. He was holding a small dumbbell and continued to curl it up and down. "If you're selling some of that stale candy, we don't want any," he said.

"I'm looking for Megan," Cindy said. Was this the right house?

"Oh. She's out back," the boy said. "And tell her it's her turn to take out the trash!"

Cindy hurried around to the backyard but didn't see anyone except Apples sitting at the bottom of a tree and looking up. Cindy looked up, and there way up in the branches was a wooden tree house. Just then Megan poked her head out of the window of the tree house and saw Cindy. "Hey! You beat me!" said Megan. "I was going to come over to your house this morning. Come on up."

Cindy just stood there and smiled.

"What's the matter?" Megan asked when Cindy didn't move.

"I don't know how to climb a tree," Cindy said sheepishly.

"You don't have to climb a tree, just climb the ladder," Megan said, and she pointed down to the tree trunk. Sure enough there were small planks of wood nailed into the tree lead-ing up to a hole in the floor of the tree house. It was a pretty high climb.

High places really weren't Cindy's favorite thing. Once, her dad had taken her on a Ferris wheel and when they had gotten to the top, it had stopped. The carriage that they were in had swung back and forth. Even though her dad kept saying they were perfectly safe, Cindy hadn't been convinced. She had clutched tight to her father and was afraid she might tip out of the little carriage. Ever since then she had gone out of her way to avoid heights.

And now here was Megan challenging her to make the climb. She certainly didn't want to look scared. Cindy took a deep breath and started to climb up. This would be Cindy's first experience with not only a ladder but also a tree house.

She made it to the top, and Megan helped pull her in.

"Pretty cool, huh?" Megan asked. "Matt and my dad built this. Now Matt's too fat to fit in here, so I took it over. I'm thinking of painting it."

"Let me guess . . . purple?" Cindy asked. She was leaning against the wall of the tree house, afraid of falling into the open hole, but Megan seemed very comfortable walking about up here. There was a little crate with some comic books stacked inside, and a flashlight hung on the wall with a piece of rope.

"Are you okay?" Megan asked.

"Sure," Cindy said. Then all at once she remembered her surprise and forgot about how high up she was.

Slowly, Cindy began to finger spell, "G-O-O-D M-O-R-N-I-N-G."

"You can sign!" Megan shrieked. "How did you learn?"

Cindy told her about the trip to the library and her mother remembering finger spelling from the Girl Scouts.

"You mean you learned to finger spell just for me?" asked Megan.

"Y-E-S," Cindy finger spelled back.

"Wow," Megan said. Then she started spelling rapidly with her fingers. Megan jumped up and down excitedly. It seemed like the whole tree house might tumble to the ground. Megan's fingers began a rapid flurry of spelling. It was very hard to follow.

"WEWILLHAVESOMUCHFUNFIN-GERSPELLINGTOGETHER."

"Whoa!" said Cindy. "Can you really spell that fast?"

"Sure can," said Megan. "Watch me." Megan started slowly with "A," but as she spelled each letter she got faster and faster. By the time she was somewhere around the letter "G," Cindy was lost. Megan was finger spelling at hyperdrive.

Megan raised one eyebrow. It looked like she wasn't finished yet.

Megan raised her *other* hand. "Watch this." And with that, she repeated the alphabet at super light speed, this time with BOTH hands facing each other. It looked as if she were finger spelling into a mirror!

"Are you really signing all the letters?" asked Cindy suspiciously.

Megan laughed. "Nah . . . I just did the letters 'A' and 'Z,'" she said. Then she laughed again. It took a second for Cindy to realize that Megan was pulling her leg.

"I'm just teasing," continued Megan.

"I want to learn how to sign *everything*," Cindy said excitedly. "Would you teach me?"

"Sure. We'll be able to talk about all sorts of things that no one will be able to know. Except my mom and dad and my gross brother Matt."

Cindy had never had her own "secret" language. But then, she'd never had a best friend like Megan, either. She was so excited about all the things she could learn with her new best friend. "How do you sign 'friend'?" Cindy asked.

Megan took one index finger, then interlocked it with the other, like two hooks. Then she turned her hands over and made the hook again with her fingers.

"Friend is like the two of us together. Stuck for life," Megan said proudly as she signed.

"Let me try!" said Cindy. "You are—" and she did her best to sign the word. "You are my friend, M-E-G-A-N," Cindy exclaimed as she signed the word ever so slowly. It was perfect.

Megan signed back, but this time without using her voice. "You are my friend, Cindy!" But instead of spelling out "Cindy," Megan held the letter "C" up to her eyes.

"What does that mean?" Cindy asked.

"That can be your name sign," Megan said proudly. "'C' for Cindy, and up by the eyes because your eyes are so big." Funny.

"What's your name sign?" Cindy asked.

Megan made the "M" letter with her finger and had it roll from her mouth. "'M' for Megan, and by my mouth because I like to talk a lot." Cindy repeated Megan's name sign.

"Cool, huh?" Megan asked.

"I only have one question," Cindy said. "How are we going to get down from here?"

Megan shook her head and rolled her eyes.

Cindy and Megan spent the rest of the afternoon up in the tree house discovering signs together.

~

salmon patties and summer plans

"WELL, YOU'RE NOT LEAVING THIS TABLE UNTIL you clean your plate. We're not going through this whole act again, Megan," said Megan's dad, David.

It was dinnertime at Megan's. Like any other home, dinnertime was a chance to share events of day, chat about school or work, or just talk about the weather. For Megan's home it was different because everyone spoke *and* signed while they sat around the table. It made for a very interesting dinner experience for the outside visitor.

On this particular night, after everyone had finished their salad, Lainee gathered the plates and went back to the kitchen to bring out the main course. Matt was telling David about baseball practice. Megan had nothing to add to that conversation. Apples was sitting at her feet and he looked just as bored as she was. Megan scrunched up her face and said, "Apples." He wagged his tail just a little.

When the kitchen door swung open, Megan's nose twitched. Something smelled odd, strange, and not at all good. Megan had a very sensitive nose. She could smell the most distant odors, like the time she had smelled the smoke from an empty lot full of weeds that was on fire . . . and it was two blocks away! She told her mother, and they had immediately called the fire department. David attributed her sense of smell to the fact that her deafness made all of her other senses sharper. Matt said it was because she had a big nose. She liked being able to smell things that other people couldn't smell right away, except for the strong perfumes that some women wore at the mall. Megan was always quick to point out those strong odors. Even when

Lainee told her she was embarrassed, Megan would grimace and hold her nose. And right now she smelled something she definitely didn't like.

"Salmon patties!" Megan said, pointing to the tray her mother was bringing in from the kitchen. Matt looked up and knew what was coming next.

"I'm not eating!" exclaimed Megan, and with that she scrunched her eyes shut.

If there was one food that made her sick, it was salmon patties. One whiff would send her into what David called "Megan shock." Whenever she didn't like what was going on, she would close her eyes and that way she wouldn't have to see anyone signing to her. If she peeked, David would often tease her by saying, "You're foaming at the mouth! Call a doctor!" Or, "You've got more tantrums in you than twenty little girls."

Megan actually had a good reason for not liking salmon patties. Once, after a school field trip to the aquarium downtown, Megan came home and found Lainee had made an unusually large batch of patties. Instead of enjoying this treat, all Megan could think of were the fish swimming back and forth in those large green tanks, opening and closing their mouths, gasping for air. Suddenly those salmon patties on the plate did the same thing. They took a life of their own. All the little pieces of salmon broke apart and swam on her plate like tiny little salmon fishes she had seen earlier that day. At one point, when Matt swallowed a particularly large patty, Megan imagined a large fish tail going down into his mouth. Slurp! Yum! Megan screamed and suddenly she was in "Megan shock" for the first time. Megan told her mother then that she had a late snack and was full. When she used the same excuse the next few times her mother served salmon patties, Lainee became suspicious. Megan finally confessed that she couldn't eat salmon patties because, for one, she hated the taste, and for two, she was afraid they would come alive and try to swim out of her mouth.

As soon as Lainee placed the platter on the

table, she tapped on Megan's shoulder. She opened her eyes. "Don't be silly and don't give me any excuses. Salmon is very good for you. Now eat up."

Megan thought she was going to be sick. What could she do? She remembered she had promised her dad that she would stop being so dramatic. She had to try her best to eat them. Megan took a deep breath and picked up her fork. Just then, for a second there, she thought she saw a fish tail flop out from the platter of patties—she couldn't do it! But she had to. She'd made a promise. She knew she would have to sit at the table the whole evening and eventually eat the little fish cakes. Matt took a big bite and smiled at her. She stuck her tongue out at him, and he just laughed. She was trapped!

Then she had a brilliant idea. Since Apples was hungry twenty-four hours a day, 365 days a year, she decided that she would help him out and feed him her salmon patties. As Lainee dished salmon patties onto her plate, Megan made an "mmmmm!" sound as if she were enjoying her food and then quietly slipped the patty onto her napkin. As she pretended to chew, she fed Apples little bits of patty. Apples chewed on the salmon like it was gum. Luckily he didn't need his teeth for these. Megan kept slipping him pieces of the fish, and he kept gumming away. This was perfect. *Everyone is so busy talking, this might actually work,* she thought.

Megan's plate was finally clean. "I'm finished!" she exclaimed.

"See, I knew you would like them," Lainee said.

"What, already?" David asked. He eyed Megan suspiciously.

She quickly changed the subject. "Hey, Matt, you think your coach will let you pitch this season?" she asked quickly. She knew Matt would talk forever about his silly baseball, and that's just what he did. When Megan was done feeding Apples, he wandered over to Matt, looking for more scraps.

"Buzz off, Apples," Matt ordered. "You smell like fish." Megan froze, expecting to be caught, but her parents didn't seem to be paying attention. They had their own agenda.

Lainee turned to David and said, "I think it's time to talk to Megan." Megan was certain it was about her and her furry companion in salmon patty crime.

"We have an idea about your plans for the summer and we'd like to talk to you about it," said David.

Megan was relieved. It didn't sound like it would be about salmon patties.

"Your dad and I have been thinking about camp for you this summer. We signed you up for Camp Ozanam," said her mother.

This was almost as terrifying as the salmon patties.

"Camp? I don't want to go to camp!" Megan pleaded. "I can't go!"

The last thing she wanted to talk about was camp. The subject had been brought up last summer, and when Megan had objected, her parents had let the whole thing pass. They'd told her maybe she was too young to go away to camp.

"Now, Megan," Lainee began, "you're old enough, and there is no reason for you not to go. You'll meet new friends and participate in fun activities. What would be wrong with that?"

"Plenty!" Megan said as she folded her arms in front of her. "Who would help Mr. Rogowski rake his lawn? Who would get Otis the cat out of the Millers' tree?" She was trying to make her case for staying home this summer. "I don't think this neighborhood could get along without me."

"But I bet they'd like to try!" Matt laughed. Megan shot him a mean look.

Megan could see Lainee was becoming frustrated. "I'm surprised at the attitude you're taking," she said. "You're not being fair."

"Fair? You're not fair," Megan shouted back. "You went ahead and planned out my whole summer without asking me first!"

"Megan. I'm sure you don't mean to speak so sharply to your mother," David scolded.

"But I don't want to go!" Megan said. She folded her arms in front of her again and pouted.

David didn't seem so cross, now that she wasn't shouting anymore, but he didn't seem too happy that Megan was still being very stubborn. "Well, Megan, you should think about changing your attitude, because you're still going to camp. It will be a good experience," said David.

Megan just sat there and looked into her lap.

Her father reached over and tapped her on her shoulder. "I promise you'll love it. Besides, it beats sitting at home all day and staring at the same walls," he said. "And your mother tells me they have camp counselors there who can sign, and maybe there will be another girl or two who is deaf like you. You never know!"

Megan didn't want to pay attention. She didn't care if the whole world signed at the camp. She didn't want to go.

"Besides," he continued, "who wants to hang around that dog with bad fish breath?" Megan's eyes widened. He knew about the fish patties!

Megan looked at her mother, who seemed

to wonder what David meant about "fish breath." But David didn't give it away. He just looked at Megan and winked. "Why don't you just go up to your room and think about it? Maybe you could even talk to your friends on the computer. I bet they'd tell you that going to camp is the best thing they ever did," said David.

Megan went up to her room and slammed the door. She flipped on her computer and plopped down in her chair. She was so upset, she didn't know what to do. She looked out the window and expected that the whole world would be mad with her. But only a gentle breeze blew her curtains.

She had a lot of thinking to do. There was no way she was going to camp. She just couldn't, and now she had to figure a way out of this mess.

CHAPTER 6

~

rolling down the sidewalk

"I MISSED WHAT YOU FINGER SPELLED, MEGAN. Where do you have to go?" Cindy asked. It was one of those bright summer days that Cindy just had to be outside playing in. She and Megan were skating down sidewalks heading toward the little row of shops on Golf Road.

"Camp!" Megan replied as she touched her index and pinkie fingers together and then brought them down on an angle. Just like a tent. Cindy still wasn't getting it. Megan sighed and finger spelled the word "C-A-M-P!"

"Camp? I've always wanted to go to camp," said Cindy. She pushed on her rear

Rollerblade foot a little harder to catch up with Megan.

"You must be out of your mind!" said Megan.

Cindy was working her hands trying to figure out a way to sign a response. As she was looking down, she wasn't paying attention to where she was skating, and CRACK! Cindy ran into a telephone pole! She was knocked right back on the ground.

The next thing she knew, Megan plopped down next to her. "Are you okay?"

Cindy was flat on her behind, with her legs out in front of her and her arms behind her. One of her Rollerblade's wheels was still spinning as it made a small squeaking sound. Cindy shook her head. She was fine. It was a good thing she was wearing her helmet. She certainly didn't expect to be hitting any telephone poles this morning.

Megan began to laugh a little.

"What's so funny?" asked Cindy.

"Oh, Cindy, I'm sorry! But it's just that when I said 'out of your mind,' you really lost yours!" said Megan as she laughed out loud.

Cindy took off her helmet. Megan's laugh was so bright and cheerful that she couldn't help but smile.

"See! You think it's funny, too," said Megan. "Come on, it's too hard to skate and sign at the same time. Let's go to Mrs. Kim's Ice-cream Shop!"

The two walked with their Rollerblades over their shoulders to the ice-cream shop, which was at the end of the row of stores on Golf Road. As they walked down the street, Megan made a point of waving hello to all the shopkeepers. It seemed as though Megan knew everybody. Cindy wondered if she could ever make friends as easily as Megan.

The door to the ice-cream shop had a little bell that tinkled when the door was opened. Cindy liked that sound. It made her think of Christmas bells. But she suddenly felt a little guilty when she realized Megan could never hear that. Then again, Megan didn't seem to be missing out on anything. Megan could certainly do a lot of things Cindy couldn't do, like climb trees and skate backward. Maybe there was nothing to feel guilty about.

Inside Mrs. Kim's, Cindy had a hard time choosing a flavor—there were so many. She had it narrowed down to either a scoop of Choco Choco Chip Cookie Delight or Pepper Minty Surprise when Megan stepped right up to the counter and ordered a "Colossus." Megan pointed to a picture above the counter of an enormous banana split. Cindy couldn't believe what she saw. It was positively overflowing with ice cream.

"You're going to eat all that?" asked Cindy as she watched Mrs. Kim start to build the "Colossus."

"Here," said Megan as she presented Cindy with a plastic spoon. "You're going to help me. There's plenty to go around! And it's my treat. I've got some leftover birthday money from my grandma Josie." Cindy still couldn't believe it. She had never eaten this much ice cream before dinner.

Megan went on. "After all, it was my signing that made you clunk your head."

There were a few tables under big umbrellas outside the ice-cream shop. Cindy and Megan sat down there while they waited for Mrs. Kim to bring over the "Colossus."

"I bet they have ice cream at camp," said Cindy.

"You gotta be kidding! Ice cream at camp?" Megan asked. "I bet it's just pork and beans or cold hot dogs and soggy marshmallows over a fire."

"Who told you that?" said Cindy.

"I asked some of my friends in the chat room," Megan explained. "They said they force you to sleep outside in a sleeping bag with bugs all over the place." She went on, "And when they run out of food, you have to eat snake soup." Megan bent her fingers like two fangs and moved it forward from her mouth to show the sign for "snake."

"I think they were just teasing you," Cindy said.

Just then Mrs. Kim brought over the "Colossus." That picture didn't do it justice . . . this was way too much ice cream in one place!

"You'd better finish it all," Mrs. Kim said

like a schoolteacher. Maybe if they didn't finish, they'd get ice-cream detention. That would be some punishment!

"Don't worry, we will," Megan said as she dug in with her spoon. Cindy followed her lead. As they were eating their ice cream, Cindy saw a group of kids walking toward them down Golf Road. There were two boys and two girls. They seemed to be about the same age as Cindy and Megan. They probably all are going to be the new classmates. The kids, laughing and kidding with one another, came up behind Megan. One of the girls had long braids that she was constantly twirling around her finger.

"Well, if it isn't Miss Megan," the girl said with a sneer. Megan saw Cindy look over her shoulder and turn around to face the kids.

"Oh hi, Charlotte," Megan said. Cindy noticed that Charlotte had no problem understanding Megan. They must be in the same class, but Megan didn't seem too happy to see this Charlotte girl.

"Did you get your final report card?"

Charlotte asked. "I got all A's and B's, so my mom gave me money to treat everyone to ice cream. I don't expect you did that well." Charlotte rolled her eyes at the other kids, and they burst out laughing.

"Shows you how much you know. I got straight A's," Megan said as she turned her back to Charlotte. Megan signed to Cindy the word S-N-O-B. Cindy couldn't believe Megan would sign that, but then she realized Charlotte couldn't possibly know what Megan said. This was one of the benefits of having a secret language.

"Whatever," Charlotte said and made a "W" by holding together her index and middle fingers of both hands. Was she making fun of Megan's signing? Charlotte led the other kids into the ice-cream parlor. Cindy could see them moving their hands, acting like they were signing. Now she was sure they were making fun of Megan. That was just plain mean. Cindy was glad Megan didn't see that.

"Who were they?" Cindy asked, trying to keep Megan's attention from those nasty kids.

"They're from school. They think they're the coolest kids, but they're the only ones who think that," Megan said. The two girls ate their ice cream in silence for a few moments.

"Anyway, about camp, I just don't get why you don't want to go," Cindy said.

"You're worse than my mother!" Megan scolded her.

Cindy wasn't used to someone with Megan's short temper. She just sat there, afraid to say anything else.

Megan thought for a moment. "Well, I wouldn't know anyone there, and the kids . . . well, they might make fun of me," she said. Cindy noticed that Megan said the words very quietly. She wondered if Megan had seen Charlotte and her friends making the signing gestures.

"Well, I'd go with you," Cindy said.

"Well, I'm not going!" said Megan.

"But you just said you wouldn't know anyone. If I went, then you'd know at least me," said Cindy. She was eating a scoop of chocolate ice cream while Megan ate the scoop of strawberry. It all made perfect sense to Cindy.

"How come you're so interested in going to camp?" Megan asked as she used her spoon to get a bit of whipped cream that had dripped over the side of the dish.

"Well, I've never been to camp, and I thought it would be fun. I guess the reason I never went was the same as you—I wouldn't know anybody there—but I was thinking now that we know each other . . ."

Her words trailed off as Charlotte and her friends came out of the shop with their ice-cream cones. They walked away without even saying good-bye to Megan. Cindy thought that was just plain rude. She hoped she wouldn't have to sit next to them in any class when school started.

Cindy went on, trying to make her case. "We could go swimming and take hikes and learn camp songs and play softball."

"And stay up all night, laughing and telling goofy stories," Megan added.

"Exactly! And we could bring our Rollerblades and skate all day," continued

Cindy. She thought she was finally convincing Megan to see her side of things.

"It's no good," Megan said.

Now what? Cindy thought.

"There would be too many trees up there for you to smash into!" Megan laughed, and snatched up the last cherry from the "Colossus."

"So you'll go?" Cindy asked eagerly. Maybe she'd convinced her friend.

Megan thought for a minute. "Sorry, I don't think so." Before Cindy could say anything else, Megan picked up the empty dish and took it back inside to Mrs. Kim.

Cindy didn't know what to do. She really liked the idea of going to camp. She was sure she could convince her parents to let her go. They always told her to get more involved in things, and this was a perfect opportunity. But like Megan, there was no way Cindy would go alone. Just then Megan came out of the ice-cream parlor and sat down to lace up her Rollerblades.

"Race you back home!" Megan said. And she was off like a flash.

"No fair!" Cindy called out as she raced to catch up with Megan. Cindy decided to drop the subject of camp for now, but she was determined to bring it up again. She was pretty sure she could convince Megan to go. Maybe all Megan needed was a little time to think it over.

~

megan's secret

"SPAGHETTI NIGHT IS MY FAVORITE NIGHT," Megan said. She and Cindy were busy chopping up vegetables for a salad while Lainee was stirring the sauce on the stove. The whole house smelled like spaghetti sauce.

Megan showed Cindy the sign for spaghetti. "Take your pinkie fingers, touch them together, then draw them apart in little waves. Just like the shape of spaghetti." Cindy tried it. "Perfect," Megan exclaimed. This particular evening, Megan was pleased to announce that Cindy was the guest of honor for dinner at the Merrill house. She even sent her another special purple invitation.

"Why don't you girls set the table?" Lainee asked.

Megan grabbed the plates and knives and forks. She handed Cindy a stack of napkins. "Follow me," she said as she led Cindy into the dining room.

They began to set the table. "So what's up with you?" Megan asked.

Cindy sighed. "I'm kind of nervous and excited at the same time," she told Megan. "I'm excited to be eating someplace other than my house. No one ever invited me over to her house for dinner without my parents!"

"That's just plain goofy," Megan said with a smile.

"Will everyone just sign at dinner? I don't know if I can keep up, even though I practiced and practiced before I came over here. Sometimes when you sign fast, I get confused."

"Relax," Megan said. "My family won't bite."

At dinner, Megan made sure Cindy sat next to her, and she kept stealing glances to make sure Cindy was following along with the flow of conversation.

"Megan tells me that your mother taught you the manual alphabet and that Megan helped you learn signs for everything else. Is that right?" asked Lainee.

Megan saw that her friend was nervous, and lent her a hand. "She's really good at signing. Show them, Cindy," said Megan proudly.

"C-I-N-D-Y," said Cindy shyly as she spelled her name.

"Now show them our name signs," Megan encouraged. Cindy did her "C" name sign and Megan's "M" name sign. Lainee and David seemed very impressed. Matt was too busy reaching for a piece of garlic bread to notice.

"And she's my friend!" said Megan. She signed the word "friend" large and clear so Cindy could see.

"That's wonderful!" said Lainee. "We're so glad you're Megan's friend," she said.

Megan could see that Cindy was smiling more after her mother's comment.

"Now aren't you glad you came over for dinner?" Megan signed to Cindy while her family wasn't looking. Cindy nodded back yes!

"Hey, Cindy. Maybe you can teach Megan some other songs besides that stupid Billy Joel song," Matt said sarcastically. He leaned down and started to sing to Apples. "I love you just the way you are . . ."

"Matt, you'd better be nice!" Megan said. She was ready to fume.

"But I love Apples because he's prettier than you," Matt continued to sing.

"Mom! Tell him to stop!" Megan yelled. She was mad at him for embarrassing her in front of her best friend. Megan wanted everything perfect for Cindy's visit, and Matt was being a jerk. She knew how to get even with him.

"Well, you've got a girlfriend, and her name is Lucy! Oh Lucy, when can I see you again?" Megan said, mocking her brother.

"Yeah? How do you know it's Lucy?" said Matt suspiciously. "Have you been eavesdropping on my phone calls, watching what I've been saying?"

"Maybe I have and maybe I haven't," Megan said. She punctuated her point by slurping up a long strand of spaghetti.

"Both of you please lower your voices," Lainee said.

Matt stuck his tongue out at Megan. Megan stuck her tongue right back at Matt.

"Cindy, your mother tells me you're excited about going to camp," said Lainee. Megan rolled her eyes. Here we go.

"Well, I guess I haven't really made up my mind yet. I was kind of hoping Megan would decide to go," Cindy said timidly.

"Don't worry, she's decided," Matt said with a sneer.

"Did not!" Megan yelled back.

"You'll have to forgive my children, Cindy," David said sternly. He shot Megan a look, which she knew meant "cut it out." "Sometimes they forget their manners." Megan knew he was serious. Both Megan and Matt quieted down after that.

"Well, I have a surprise for you two," Lainee said as she looked over to Cindy and Megan with a smile. "I called your mother, Cindy, and she said you could spend the night tonight. Sort of practice for camp."

Megan couldn't believe what her mother was saying. She wanted to jump up from the table and run and hide, but she knew her father would be really mad.

"Thanks, Mrs. Merrill," Cindy said. "This will be fun!" Cindy brushed her first two fingers against her nose and brought them down to tap her other two fingertips. The sign for "fun." But Megan wasn't convinced Cindy spending the night would really be fun.

After dinner, the family played Monopoly and made Cindy feel right at home. Megan couldn't believe this. How come I never get a say in anything? she wondered. She didn't really want to play Monopoly, and just went through the motions. Everyone is so busy playing and laughing, they don't even notice. She felt like shouting or running out to the tree house. Instead, she sat there and played the game. She was worried about what Cindy might discover later that night.

When it was time for bed, Lainee had the trundle bed pulled out ready for Cindy. She even gave Cindy a pair of Megan's pajamas.

After the girls had brushed their teeth and changed into their pj's, they settled into bed.

Lainee and David poked their heads in the door. "We'd tell you to turn out the lights and go to bed but we'd be wasting our breath," David said with a smile.

"Good night, girls," Lainee said. "Try to get some sleep." They closed the door.

"Wow, my first sleepover! My parents must be missing me for sure!" said Cindy. "I guess this will be good practice for them if I go to camp."

Megan sat up in her bed. She was very anxious.

"What's wrong?" asked Cindy with a quizzical look.

"Nothing," Megan said.

"Liar."

"Am not," Megan yelled back.

"Gee, I was only kidding around," Cindy said.

"Well, I don't want anyone to sleep over," Megan said.

Cindy sat there in silence. Megan could tell she was instantly hurt. This was coming out all wrong.

"Do you want me to leave?" Cindy finally asked.

Megan frowned. "No," she said quietly. Now she could see Cindy was really confused. Megan got out of bed and began pacing back and forth across the room. As she did she had to kick some clothes and toys out of the way to clear a path. Cindy sat there pulling the covers up closer to her. She looked as if she was afraid to say anything.

"If I tell you something, you promise you won't tell anyone ever, ever, ever?" Megan asked.

"I promise," Cindy said quickly.

Megan crossed back over to her bed. She took a moment to gather her thoughts. "This is the real reason I'm afraid the kids at camp will make fun of me." With that, she pulled a tattered old purple blanket from underneath her pillow. It certainly wasn't a bright purple like the rest of the things in her room. Megan was suddenly aware that her prized possession looked very old and had been washed about a hundred times. The blanket had seen better days.

"You can't go to camp because of a blanket?" Cindy asked.

"It's my special blanket," Megan said. She couldn't even look Cindy in the eye when she talked. "I've had it forever. I never sleep without it."

"Oh. Well, gee, I have a teddy bear that I sleep with," Cindy said. If she was trying to make Megan feel better, it didn't work.

There was more to Megan's secret.

"I need my blanket when I sleep and when I . . ." Megan slowly stuck her thumb in her mouth.

Cindy didn't seem to understand this at first. Then she widened her eyes and she slowly nodded her head. "You still suck your thumb?" Cindy called out.

"Why don't you just shout it out to the whole neighborhood?" Megan was mortified.

"Sorry," Cindy said.

Megan got back up from the bed and began pacing again. "I know I'm too old to have a blanket and suck my thumb, but I can't help it," she said.

There, she had finally said it out loud. It was Megan's biggest secret, but admitting it to Cindy had made a little part of Megan feel good.

"Well, I used to suck my thumb, too," Cindy said.

"Right, when you were a baby," Megan responded.

"I don't think it was that long ago that I stopped."

"Really?" Megan was a little encouraged to hear this.

"Yeah."

"So how did you stop?" Megan had to know. She felt like she was the only nine-year-old in the whole world who still sucked her thumb.

"I guess I just decided to," Cindy said with a shrug. Megan didn't offer up an argument, and encouraged Cindy to go on. "And that's no reason not to go to camp. I mean, even if you did still do that . . . who would know? Everyone will be asleep. And I'll take my teddy bear, so maybe if you take your blanket, it won't seem so bad."

"I guess." Megan shrugged.

"It can be our secret together," Cindy said.

Megan began to think this through a little bit. "Maybe, just maybe, if I go to camp, it will force me to stop."

"That's a great idea," Cindy said. "I bet after four weeks at camp, you'll be cured for sure."

"And I bet my brother will be glad not to hear Billy Joel for four weeks!"

And then Megan looked at Cindy as if they had the same thought.

"And no smelly Apples!" They said the words at the same time together. They couldn't help but laugh out loud.

"So we would have a good time together, right?" Cindy asked.

"Of course! We'll have a . . ." and then Megan signed without speaking.

Cindy seemed stumped. "What's this mean?" asked Cindy as she repeated the sign, with both palms facing outward like she was ready to hit a volleyball.

"It means fantastic, wonderful, marvelous!" Megan explained.

"Then you'll go?" Cindy asked.

Megan thought for a minute. Was Cindy actually holding her breath? Megan picked up the tattered old purple blanket and shoved it back under her pillow. "I'll go!" Megan said.

After a little more chattering, Cindy yawned and drifted off to sleep. Megan wasn't far behind. Before she did, she pulled out just a little bitty corner of her purple blanket from under her pillow. *No sense giving it up all at once,* she thought.

CHAPTER 8

~

countdown to camp

ONCE CINDY AND MEGAN TOLD THEIR
parents that they would both be going away to
camp, things kicked into high gear. Before she
knew it, it was the day before Cindy was leaving and she and Megan had one last trip to
the mall to make. It was one of those "mega-
malls," the kind with hundreds of shops and
tons of places to eat. Lainee drove the girls
over.

"This is like my neighborhood," said
Megan proudly as she pointed out the stores
to Cindy. "I know everyone who works here!"

Lainee told the girls not to talk to strangers.
She instructed them to meet in two hours in

front of the main entrance where they came into the mall. Cindy watched as Megan folded the envelope of money that Lainee gave her and tucked it in the waistband of her shorts. That reminded Cindy to pat her front pocket to make sure she still had the money her mother had given her. It was there.

"You sure we won't get lost?" said Cindy as they walked down the mall. "It's such a big mall!"

The mall ceilings towered over her head. There were three different corridors with stores as far as the eye could see going off in three different directions. She'd never seen anything this big before.

"Oh, it'll be fine," said Megan. "We can shop around. And if we can't find anything in the rest of the mall, I know one place where we can definitely buy our stuff for camp."

Cindy followed Megan as she took her to all the stores she shopped at with her mother. In Tannebaum's, the big department store, Cindy noticed instead of summer clothes, all the clothes on sale were for school. "Looks like we can shop for school, too," she said.

"Who wants to think about school now?" said Megan as she pulled Cindy by the hand out of the department store.

"Right," said Cindy. There will be plenty of time to think about school later.

Finally after walking what seemed like miles, Cindy and Megan came upon Powell's, a huge discount outlet store. Megan said that of all places that they searched for camp clothing, Powell's would be the best place to go. Cindy couldn't believe the racks and racks of clothing all shoved together and strewn about. It looked a little bit like Megan's room, but Cindy didn't want to tell her that. "Where are we going to start? There are so many clothes," said Cindy.

Just then Megan took off running excitedly down to the main checkout stand. "Follow me," she said over her shoulder.

Cindy ran down the aisle after Megan. She noticed that each salesperson waved or smiled at Megan as she passed by. It was just like all the shopkeepers on Golf Road. Somehow being with Megan made Cindy feel a little popular.

"There's Claire!" Megan said, pointing out one of the salespersons. Before they got close to Claire, Megan tugged on Cindy's shirt-sleeve and pulled her in close. She then spelled out P-E-R-F-U-M-E and scrunched up her nose. Cindy didn't understand what she meant, but when she got close to Claire, she knew. Claire was a pretty woman who wore way too much perfume. Cindy watched Megan scrunch up her nose again. She had to stop herself from laughing.

"So, what are you looking for today, Megan?" asked Claire.

"Camp clothes!" said Megan excitedly. "Me and my best friend are going to camp!"

"Well, we just got a new shipment of shorts in some really cool colors I know you'll like!" said Claire. "Come here and take a look!"

Claire had turned her back away from Cindy and Megan.

"What did you say?" said Megan.

Before Claire could answer, Cindy jumped

in and began signing. She was very eager to help her best friend. "She said they have shorts in some awesome new colors." Cindy was proud she could translate so quickly for Megan.

But suddenly Megan was frowning. "I didn't ask you to help me, Cindy," Megan said angrily.

"But I thought you said you didn't know what she said—" Before Cindy could finish, Megan interrupted her.

"That doesn't mean you need to jump in!" Megan said loudly, then turned away. Cindy noticed that Claire was trying not to stare. But she also knew that Claire could hear everything because Megan was talking very loud. Cindy could feel her face flush with embarrassment.

Claire directed the girls to some racks of shorts just one aisle over. Then she excused herself to help other customers. Before she left she made a point of telling Megan to call her if she had any questions. Claire said this with a very loud voice and over-enunciated lips.

"Megan, aren't these purple shorts the

coolest?" Cindy said as she held up a pair of long purple shorts against her waist to see if they would fit. She was hoping the sight of a pair of purple shorts might make Megan smile. But Megan didn't respond. Was Megan really mad at her? Maybe there was something lost in the translation of signs. "Megan? Don't you like these shorts?"

"I don't know," said Megan as she flipped through the shorts without really looking at them.

"Okay. What's the matter?"

"I'm fine," said Megan. Now she was flipping through the shorts faster.

"Well, you're not acting like you're fine."

"Excuse me," said Megan. "But I can do things by myself."

"But you didn't understand what she was saying, and I was just using my sign language to help!" said Cindy.

Megan shook her head and went back to looking at more shorts. Cindy didn't know what she was doing wrong. This trip to the mall was turning out not to be so much fun after all. She walked around to stand in front of Megan so that she could see her signing.

"Well, I'm sorry," said Cindy. "I was just trying to be helpful." She didn't even want to look Megan in the eye. "I don't think you're being very fair." It took a lot for Cindy to say that, but she just had to.

Then she glanced over at the clock on the wall. They only had ten minutes before they had to meet Lainee, and they hadn't bought a thing! "Look at the time," she said, pointing at the clock.

Megan saw the clock and quickly grabbed some shorts and threw them at Cindy. "Hurry up! My mom will flip out if we spent all this time and didn't get anything for camp!"

Without really looking at what she was buying, Cindy took the shorts over to the counter where Claire was helping other customers. She paid for them, then raced out of the store with Megan. When they got to the front entrance of the mall, they found Lainee looking at her watch.

"You girls have lots to do before you leave for camp," said Lainee as she rushed them to the car.

Cindy fastened her seat belt as Lainee backed the car out of the parking space. Cindy noticed that Megan wasn't saying anything as she buckled up, so she decided to be quiet right along with her.

"Cindy, did you enjoy Powell's?" asked Lainee.

"I guess," Cindy said. "It's a really big mall, though."

"Well, with Megan as your guide, you'll have no problem finding your way around."

Cindy watched Megan look at her mother speaking in the rearview mirror. That's how they could communicate when Megan was in the backseat. Megan looked out the window, so Cindy did the same.

At the next light, Lainee turned around and signed and spoke at the same time to the two girls, "Is everything okay back there?"

"Everything is fine," said Megan as she rolled her eyes. But they weren't really fine, because Cindy and Megan didn't speak or sign to each other for the entire way home.

~

the right choice?

"I GUESS SOMEONE IS TOO EXCITED TO SLEEP in this morning," said Lainee. By the time Lainee came in to wake her up, Megan was already fully dressed and sitting on her bags, ready to go.

"Maybe I'll take a stab at cleaning up this disaster area while you're gone," Lainee said as she crossed to the windows to open them.

Megan did a last-minute check of her bags. She hoped she hadn't forgotten anything.

"Camp is going to be fun, isn't it?" said Lainee as she sat down on the bed next to Megan.

Megan looked at her. "Aren't we going to be late?" she asked.

"Don't worry," said Lainee as she pointed to Megan's big purple clock on the wall. It read 7:00. "We still have an hour."

Megan sat there and played with the bracelet on her wrist. It was a braid of multi-colored strings that she had made herself. She sighed.

"Okay, what's wrong?" Lainee asked. "Ever since you came back from the mall yesterday you've been moping around. I would have thought you'd be more excited about going away with Cindy."

"She's always butting in and trying to do things for me," said Megan. She got up from the bed and walked over to her desk. She was looking for some pens and pencils to take with her to camp. "If I'm going to this stupid camp, I wish I was going by myself."

"You don't mean that," said Lainee.

"Yes, I do." Megan crossed back to her bag with her pens and pencils.

Lainee patted the bed. Megan sat down next to her.

"There's nothing wrong with people wanting to help," said Lainee. "But, then, you have to want or need it, don't you?"

"How can I tell her I don't want it? I told her yesterday, and she got all mad," said Megan. "She said I wasn't being fair."

"Remember last week when we saw Mrs. Hammer from down the street having a hard time getting up the ramp with her wheelchair? Do you remember what I did?" asked Lainee.

"You helped her up . . . ," said Megan.

"But do you remember what I did before that?" said Lainee.

She thought for a moment, but couldn't remember.

"I asked her if she wanted help," said Lainee.

"But Cindy never asked me if I wanted help. She just did it!" protested Megan.

"You have to tell her nicely that when you need her help, you'll ask for it," said Lainee. "And really, isn't she just trying to be nice?"

Was Mom right? She always seemed to know the right thing to say. Maybe she was right.

"You mean I need to help *her?*" asked Megan.

"I think you know the answer to that," said Lainee. She smiled at her.

Megan thought for a moment, then hugged Lainee hard.

David entered the room. "What's this? Don't I get a hug like that?"

"Oh, Dad," Megan said as she hugged him. "I'm going to miss you so much."

Matt appeared at the door, rubbing sleep out of his eyes, and his hair stuck out in every direction. He obviously had just woken up. "Can you guys keep it down? It's school vacation you know," he said, half-yawning.

"How about giving your sister a proper good-bye? She's going away for the first time by herself today," said David.

"I've only heard about it a million times," Matt said. "Good-bye, sis. Have fun at camp." He tossed her a small brown paper bag. Megan caught the bag and looked inside. It was full of bubble gum in all flavors! In all the excitement of packing, Megan had forgotten about the most important thing—bubble gum!

"Take your time and don't hurry back!" Matt said, then left the room.

Lainee smiled and glanced at the clock. "Well, if you're so eager, I guess we should go."

David helped carry Megan's bags to the car. Megan picked up her backpack and looked back at her room one last time. She wondered what color the camp bunkhouse would be. Just then, she saw it . . . her purple blanket. She almost forgot that! She ran over to the bed, rolled it up in a ball, and stuffed it into the bottom of her backpack. No one was going to see that. Now she could go.

Outside, Megan opened the door to the car. Sitting in the backseat was Apples.

"Mom! Does Apples have to go with us to the bus stop? His breath is going to stink up the car!" said Megan with a groan.

But she didn't really mean that. She was actually glad Apples was coming along. Even though he did have stinky breath, she was going to miss him. When her mom wasn't looking, she gave Apples a small hug. "Who's going to give you treats when I'm away, Apples?" she signed without speaking.

When the car pulled up to the YMCA parking lot, Megan could see it was full of parents and kids. It looked like the first day of school, except everyone was wearing shorts and T-shirts and they all had suitcases and duffel bags. Suddenly her heart began to race.

"Did you bring enough hearing aid batteries?" Lainee asked as she helped get Megan's bag out of the car.

"Mom, I'm old enough to know better," said Megan. She was trying her best not to look anxious.

"Just checking . . . ," said Lainee. Megan quickly patted the side of her backpack to make sure the batteries were there.

Just then Cindy and her parents walked up.

"Hi," said Megan.

"Hi," said Cindy.

Megan noticed that Cindy wasn't really looking at her.

"Well, it looks like you girls are ready to go,

doesn't it?" said Lainee. She leaned down and hugged Megan. Lainee began to cry.

"Mom . . . ," Megan said as her mother squeezed her tight.

As if on cue, Cindy's mother leaned down to Cindy, gave her a hearty hug, and started to cry, too.

"Mothers," Megan signed to Cindy.

"Really," Cindy signed back. She smiled a little.

Then Megan rolled her eyes and shrugged. Cindy rolled her eyes and shrugged back. It was almost as if they were twins, looking in a mirror.

"See you in four weeks," said Cindy's father. "Now you'd better get on the bus!"

Megan and Cindy hopped onto the bus. All the other kids were on board, chatting away. There were two empty seats in the back, and they scrambled to sit down. Megan looked out the window as all the parents lined up and waved at the bus.

After what seemed like minutes, Megan decided to break the ice. "Oh, I forgot, I have something for you," she said as she reached into her backpack. "Here!" Megan held up a brightly colored bracelet just like the one she was wearing. "This is for you."

"What is it for?" asked Cindy.

Megan grabbed it out of Cindy's hand and tied it around Cindy's wrist. It fit perfectly. "Duh! This is for our friendship. You're my best friend, remember?" said Megan as she tied the last knot.

"Really?" said Cindy. Megan watched Cindy roll the bracelet around her wrist.

"It's beautiful," said Cindy. Now she was really smiling.

"Best friends forever!" said Megan.

Megan elbowed Cindy and pointed out the bus window. They waved one last time at their parents. Both of their moms were wiping their eyes and blowing their noses. It looked like all the moms were crying.

Megan turned to Cindy and pretended to cry. Cindy joined in until both girls burst out laughing.

"This is going to be the most fun trip in the

whole world!" said Megan.

"Best friends?" asked Cindy as she signed the words and held on to her bracelet.

"Forever!" signed Megan proudly. "BFF!"

And the bus rumbled out of the parking lot onto the highway.

CHAPTER 10

~

ozanam at last!

"EVERYBODY OUT!" SAID RUTHIE, THE CAMP counselor, clipboard in hand. Cindy and Megan gathered their belongings and stumbled out of the bus. They finally had arrived at Camp Ozanam.

The five-hour bus ride felt like it would never end. Cindy had fallen asleep only an hour after they had left home. Suddenly someone on the bus said, "Look, cows!"

Cindy heard that and woke up with a startle, which woke up Megan, since she was leaning on Cindy's shoulder. "What's the sign for 'cow'?" Cindy asked.

Megan held her thumbs up to the temples

of her head and extended her pinkie fingers. She shook them back and forth just like a cow's horns. That made perfect sense to Cindy.

"I hope they make chocolate milk!" another kid called out. Everyone laughed.

They were definitely far from home. In fact, there weren't any homes anywhere. Just mountains and trees. The bus was traveling along a winding two-lane road. Cindy loved seeing this many trees. Megan reached over and pushed the window down. Soon all the kids on the bus did the same.

Finally, someone up at the front of the bus hollered out, "We're here." All the kids sat up and peered up ahead.

"Another cow?" Megan asked Cindy.

"Nope," she answered. "It's the camp!"

"It's about time!" Megan said.

The main entrance was an archway made out of logs. Next to the archway was a big American flag flapping in the wind. And next to the flag, in big, log cabin-style letters, was a sign that said CAMP OZANAM. Below that was another sign that said, THE BIGGEST LITTLE CAMP IN AMERICA.

There were a few other buses that had already arrived. The kids from those buses were already in the parking lot. Down the hill from the parking lot, Cindy could see a crystal blue lake. A few sailboats were crisscrossing the calm waters. She took a deep breath. The air seemed so much sweeter. She was really here.

"Rank and file, fall out!" Ruthie ordered as she stepped onto the bus. It wasn't so much a command as it was a cheery, good-spirited order. Ruthie was a tall, lanky, eighteen-year-old girl who had long black hair tied in a ponytail, and light brown eyes. And those teeth! Cindy marveled at Ruthie's two perfect rows of white teeth. She had never seen such white teeth except on TV actors. Even as she was thinking that, Megan signed, "Bright teeth, huh?"

"Basso, Dyas, Tannebaum!" Ruthie called out. As the campers stepped off the bus they were given name tags to stick to their shirts.

Cindy elbowed Megan and spelled the name "Tannebaum" and wondered if the young girl who had raised her hand was related to the Tannebaum family that had the store at the mega-mall.

"Calicchio!"

"Present," Cindy called out. She stood up and made her way to the aisle.

"Woodman, Merrill!" Ruthie barked. "Merrill? Where's Merrill?"

Megan was busy looking out the window at the sailboats and all the other kids getting off the other buses.

"Merrill?" yelled Ruthie one more time.

Cindy felt trapped. She wanted to help Megan, but she also remembered about her asking for help. But she didn't want Megan to get yelled at by Ruthie.

"That's Megan back there," Cindy finally volunteered. "She's deaf." Cindy knew Megan couldn't see what she said, so maybe it would be all right to help like that just this one time.

Ruthie walked up to Megan. "You're Megan Merrill?" asked Ruthie.

Megan understood her perfectly and nodded.

"Welcome to Camp Ozanam," said Ruthie. Cindy's jaw dropped when she saw that Ruthie signed as she spoke. "We got a call about you coming up. I've been assigned to be your camp counselor."

"You sign?" Megan asked.

"My sister is deaf, too, but I don't get enough practice since she's away at college in Washington, D.C.," said Ruthie. "So, I'm going to have to depend on you to help me refresh my skills." Ruthie stuck out her hand. "Deal?"

"Deal!" said Megan. Cindy followed Ruthie and Megan off the bus.

"Maybe camp won't be so bad after all," Megan told Cindy.

What other surprises were in store at Camp Ozanam?

~

hot pink cabin rules!

MEGAN AND CINDY, ALONG WITH SOME OF the other kids, were led down a trail toward the wooden bunkhouse cabins. There were so many new smells up here. Cedar wood chips on the ground. The breeze coming off the lake. The pine trees. Megan's sense of smell was working on overload!

There were several of the bunkhouse cabins all around the camp. In each one, a different group of kids was unpacking.

"Megan, Cindy . . . this is your home for the next three weeks," Ruthie said. "Hurry up and settle in." She walked off with the other kids.

The girls clumped up the steps with their

bags. A wooden sign right next to the door said, HOT PINK CABIN.

"At least it's not Hot Purple Cabin," Cindy teased Megan.

Inside were four sets of bunk beds. Megan felt the bunkhouse smelled a little bit like her attic. Musty. She noticed sleeping bags and backpacks on most of the bunks. The only empty bunk bed was next to the door.

"Let's grab this one," said Megan as she hoisted her backpack onto the upper bunk. "I'll take the top bunk, and you take the lower bunk." She wondered if Cindy liked sleeping up on top, but since she didn't say anything, she went ahead and put her bag up there.

Just then she felt the cabin floor rumble. She turned to see a group of girls had filed into the cabin. They were all talking up a storm. Megan tried to take notice of their name tags, but it was difficult because everyone was moving around so much. She was also having a hard time following the conversations back and forth. They all seemed to be talking at once. Finally she zeroed in on one girl who was asking why the cabin was called the "Hot Pink Cabin."

The girls had finally settled down on their bunks. Now it would be easy to read their lips.

"I think it's sexist," said a girl who's name tag read ARIELLE. As she flopped down on her bunk bed the beaded cornrows in her hair clanked together. Did those things hurt?

"Well, it's way better than a baby blue cabin!" said Rachel. Megan noticed she had red hair tucked under a baseball cap and was bouncing a basketball as she spoke. But because Rachel wore braces on her teeth, Megan had to ask Cindy what she said. Braces were a lip-reader's nightmare.

"Earth to Pink Ladies, Earth to Pink Ladies . . . hello?" said Barb. She had curly blond hair, pretty earrings, and painted fingernails. Megan had never seen a girl her age with painted fingernails. For some reason, Barb bobbed her head up and down as she spoke. It was making Megan dizzy watching her lips. "Pink is, like, for girls and blue is, like, for boys!" said Barb.

A short girl named Wendy, who stood next to Barb, just blew bubbles with her bubble gum. POP! She didn't say anything. Megan wondered what flavor she was chewing.

Finally, a girl with a name tag that read JESSIE said, "I think pink is such a depressing color." The other girls giggled. Jessie was dressed all in black—black shorts, black T-shirt, black sneakers and socks, and even black-rimmed glasses. *If pink was a depressing color,* Megan thought, *then what was black?*

All eyes then turned to Megan and Cindy, who had just begun to unpack. Megan had a very keen sense of when someone was staring at her, and at this particular moment, she was very aware.

"What a group!" Megan finger spelled to Cindy. Cindy just nodded quietly and continued to unpack.

Megan had to remind herself that her mother had told her the fun of camp was sharing a room with complete strangers who eventually became your friends no matter how weird or different they seemed.

Rachel bounced her basketball over to Cindy and Megan. "Hey, wazup?" she said in between bounces.

"Hey," Megan said right back. "I'm Megan, and this is Cindy." Cindy just waved.

Arielle came up behind Rachel. "Is she the deaf girl?"

"I am," Megan said. "And I can also read lips."

Arielle turned completely red. Megan stuck out her hand to shake. "Gotcha!"

Arielle laughed. All the girls came over to introduce themselves. They all began chattering together. It was almost too much for Megan to take at one time. She looked over to Cindy. She seemed just as overwhelmed.

"So, what, are you two, like, friends and all?" Barb asked.

"BFF. Best friends forever," Megan said, and signed.

"You use sign language, huh?" Rachel asked. "I saw that on TV once. That was way cool." Megan was getting used to her braces.

"It's fun," Cindy said as she signed.

"You shoot baskets? We're gonna need a guard," Rachel said, sizing up Megan and Cindy.

Barb interrupted. "Okay, is it just me or are there, like, some cute guys here or what?"

Rachel started dribbling around the cabin. Megan only got every other word that she was saying.

"Boys . . . stupid. They just wanna sit . . . and . . . wrestle or play lame video . . . I bet I could beat . . . them in one on one."

Even though she missed a lot of the words, Megan knew what she was saying just from the expression on her face and what she was doing.

"I'm kind of hungry," Wendy said. "Aren't they supposed to feed us when we get hungry?"

Jessie rolled her eyes. "This is going to be a long summer."

The girls continued chatting away. Megan liked these girls a lot more than the girls from school. Even the normally shy Cindy seemed to be getting along with them.

Suddenly Megan was startled when she heard a very high screeching sound. "What is that?" she asked. The sound hurt her ears. The other girls began to laugh.

"It's a whistle," said Cindy.

Was she laughing, too?

Suddenly Ruthie popped her head into the cabin. "Didn't you girls hear my whistle for dinner?" she said, then she looked at Megan and signed as she spoke. "Not you, Megan. I know you didn't hear it."

Megan looked at Ruthie and then got the most brilliant idea to get even with Cindy for laughing at her. "That's right, I didn't hear it," Megan said innocently. She grabbed Cindy and pulled her to her side. "Cindy will have to be my ears here at camp. She'll follow me everywhere and tell me every time the whistle blows for meals."

"But I thought you could hear a little bit . . ." said Cindy.

Megan gave her a little jab with her elbow. "Cindy here thinks I can hear a little bit, but I really can't," said Megan. "If you need to tell me anything or need to find me, look for Cindy first and then she'll come find me!" Megan tried her best not to give away the joke.

"No problem, Megan," said Ruthie. "That's what being at camp is all about. It's about being a team."

Megan was pleased with herself. Now Cindy would have the extra responsibility of listening for Megan while Megan could pretend she couldn't hear a thing. That way Megan could get away with all sorts of tricks.

"And judging from what I see in this cabin, you girls could use a lesson in team cleaning!" said Ruthie as she surveyed the room.

"Just like my mother," Megan signed.

"Your mother is right," Ruthie signed back. Megan had forgot for a second that Ruthie understood her signing.

The only bunk that wasn't messy was the one that wasn't occupied. Ruthie told them that the girl who was going to occupy that bunk would be arriving later that night, after dinner.

"Since Megan probably has better eyes than the rest of you, she'll be responsible to make sure the entire cabin is straight and clean," said Ruthie. "Right, Megan?"

This was all wrong. Her joke had backfired. Now she would have responsibilities far greater than the other girls would in the cabin.

"And speaking of being responsible," continued Ruthie as she spoke and signed, "each cabin here at Ozanam is responsible for coming up with their own camp song, which we take turns singing every morning before breakfast. So, this weekend your assignment is to come up with a camp song and have it ready for breakfast Monday morning."

A song? By Monday? That was only two days away. Megan saw the rest of the girls were staring in disbelief like her.

"Well then, it's time for dinner," said Ruthie as she motioned to the girls to file out of the cabin. "Move out before your dinner gets cold."

Megan was the last one to leave the cabin

when Ruthie stopped her for a second. Ruthie motioned for Cindy to go on ahead while she spoke to Megan.

"I remember what it was like for my sister growing up," signed Ruthie. "I used to help her out often when she didn't understand what people were saying."

"But I don't need any special help," protested Megan.

"That's what I thought," said Ruthie. "I knew you weren't telling the truth about Cindy helping you."

Megan felt like the cartoon cat that swallowed the canary and just got caught.

"I am going to treat you just like anybody else," said Ruthie. "Deal?" She held out her hand.

"Deal!" said Megan.

"Now hurry up and get to dinner. You've got some snake stew waiting for you," said Ruthie.

"Gross!" said Megan.

Although Megan had no idea where the Meet Hall was, she followed her nose. It wasn't hard to get lost when the smell of hot dogs was your guide.

Dinner wasn't as bad as Megan thought it would be. It was like a typical school lunch with a choice of hamburgers or hot dogs, vegetables, and either Jell-O or a brownie for dessert. But instead of mean-looking ladies with hairnets, the kids at the camp took turns serving food. And here at Ozanam no one needed to bring money to pay for dinner. Later on, Ruthie told Megan that it was because meals were part of the package.

By the time dinner was over, it had gotten dark. Megan and Cindy used the flashlights their parents bought them for camp to find their way back to the cabin. Barb led the other girls from the Hot Pink Cabin on a mission to check out the boys' cabins on the other side of the camp. Megan got comfortable in her upper bunk. She'd much rather dive into the stack of comics she brought with her then run off chasing after boys.

"I'm going to brush my teeth," said Cindy as she poked her head up onto Megan's bunk.

"Keep an eye out for snakes. They crawl out of the pipes!" said Megan.

Megan laughed to herself when Cindy picked up Rachel's baseball bat to take into the bathroom. "I'm just kidding!" said Megan. "There aren't any snakes in the pipes."

Cindy still looked unsure as she walked outside to go to the communal bathroom house.

Megan started to read when she felt the door to the cabin slam. "How were the boys?" she asked. Megan looked down over her bunk. She assumed it was one of the other bunkmates, but when she looked around, no one was there, either.

Suddenly she caught a faint whiff of perfumed soap. When she turned to look down her side of the cabin to the bed next to hers, she saw a skinny blond girl unpacking her things. *Must be the new bunkmate,* Megan thought as she climbed down onto the floor to check her out.

Something about the girl caught her eye.

Unlike Arielle, she didn't have a crazy hairstyle. Hers was straight and blond. She didn't
have braces like Rachel, and it didn't seem like
she was a head bobber, like Barb. She didn't
wear any makeup, and it didn't look like she
had any pimples like Wendy. And most of all,
she wore purple shorts and a red T-shirt, as if
she had shopped at Powell's.

"Hi, I'm Megan. Who are you?" she said.

The blond girl kept on unpacking and
ignored Megan. Megan tried once again. "Hi,
I'm Megan." But there was still no reply.

This was infuriating. Worse than any goofy-
looking bunkmate would be a bunkmate who
was rude. She jumped off her bunk and
walked over to the girl. She stomped on the
floor and made her signs big and clear. "Who
are you?"

The girl turned around as if startled. Her
eyes opened very wide.

"Hi! I'm Lizzie," said the girl. She was signing. "I'm sorry I didn't hear you." She looked
at Megan. "I'm deaf."

Megan's heart leaped. The idea of another

bunkmate, in HER cabin, who was deaf, was too good to be true. Megan signed, "I'm M-E-G-A-N. I'm deaf, too!" Megan's hand began to fly at light speed as she asked Lizzie all sorts of questions. And Lizzie's hands flew at light speed right back. She was a fluent signer just like Megan.

"Where are you from?" asked Megan.

"Long Grove," said Lizzie.

"That's on the other side of town from my house!" said Megan. "Is this your first time here?"

"Oh, no," said Lizzie. "This is my second time."

"How come you don't wear hearing aids?" asked Megan.

"My parents said I don't need them," said Lizzie.

"Do you speak, too?" asked Megan.

"I just sign," said Lizzie. "I go to ISD," and then Lizzie spelled out Illinois School for the Deaf. "It's deaf kids only, but my parents sent me here to hang around hearing kids during the summer."

"Wow!" said Megan. She had never met a girl who went to an all-deaf school before.

The two girls sat, signing away, getting to know each other. They talked about Ruthie, the other cabin mates, and their families.

"This is going to be the coolest summer ever!" said Megan.

Suddenly the door to the cabin slammed shut. Megan felt that and turned around. It was Cindy.

"Your turn," said Cindy. "No snakes so far," she continued. "Just big gross bugs that fly around the lights and crawl on the floor. Yuck!"

Megan grabbed Lizzie by the hand and dragged her to Cindy. "Cindy! This is our new bunkmate. Her name is Lizzie! She's going to be our new best friend here, at camp!"

Megan saw Cindy mouth the question, "Best friend?"

"Hi, I'm L-I-Z-Z-I-E," signed Lizzie. "I'm deaf. Nice to meet you. Are you deaf, too?"

"Isn't that great?" Megan asked Cindy. "We can all sign together!" As Lizzie continued to sign away, Megan caught a quick glance at Cindy.

Megan could tell from the look on Cindy's face that she didn't seem too happy.

~

the cabin song

"WHERE'S MEGAN?" BARB ASKED AS SHE bobbed her head slightly. "It's not fair that we have to, like, work on our song and she's off in her own little deaf world with Lizzie."

"They're probably helping Ruthie with her sign language," Cindy said. They were sitting on their bunks with pads of paper and pens in front of them.

"How come you're not with them? Aren't you in their little deaf world, too, BFF?" said Rachel sarcastically.

For the first time Cindy wondered if she was part of Megan's deaf world. Lizzie had arrived at Camp Ozanam on Friday night, and

Megan had spent all Saturday and Sunday hanging out with her. It was almost as if Megan had forgotten that Cindy was her best friend.

"I don't know . . . ," said Cindy as her voice trailed off.

On the first morning after they had arrived, Megan, Cindy, and Lizzie had gone to the Meet Hall after breakfast to see what activities were posted for the day on the camp bulletin board. The Meet Hall was an old barn converted into a huge space with rows and rows of tables and benches. It was the center of Camp Ozanam.

The Meet Hall was also the Dining Hall. After the dishes and tables were clear, everyone was invited back in to use the Meet Hall for whatever activity was planned there—whether it was classes in art, computer games, dance lessons, or just meeting other campers.

That first day, Megan had signed up Cindy and Lizzie for all sorts of activities. First it would be swimming, then gymnastics after lunch, and later an art class. As the day went on, Megan and Lizzie had begun to sign faster and faster to each other. At one point, Megan and Lizzie had been so involved in a conversation, it was nearly impossible for Cindy to follow what they were saying, and Megan hadn't helped her—at all.

By breakfast on Sunday morning, Megan became so involved in a conversation with Lizzie that she began to sign without speaking.

After a few minutes of asking Megan "Huh?" or "What's that mean?" Cindy gave up and went back to the cabin. She pulled out one of her books and started to read, but she couldn't concentrate. Her best friend had deserted her.

She must have been in there for a while, because when the other girls came into the cabin to figure out what song they would sing tomorrow at breakfast, Cindy noticed that it was already four o'clock. The day had flown by.

"I think the whole song thing is stupid," said Jessie.

"Yeah," agreed Wendy as she popped a bubble. "Whoever heard of making nine-year-olds write songs?"

"Well," said Rachel, "somebody better come up with something, because I don't want to look like a loser!"

"But Ruthie said it wasn't a competition," blurted out Arielle.

"Tell that to everybody else," said Rachel right back.

"I'm sorry, but I can't write without my computer," Barb said.

"Oh, no, we're going to lose," Wendy whined.

Everyone began arguing so furiously that they all ended up talking over one another. No one could understand a thing. It looked like they would never write their song. Then Cindy got an idea. She wasn't sure if she should say anything, but why not try? "I have a song," she volunteered quietly.

"Huh?" said Barb.

"Wow, I think that's the first time I heard you talk without Megan being around,"

Rachel joked. A few of the girls giggled. Cindy wished she hadn't said anything.

"What's your song?" Jessie asked suspiciously.

"It's a song we learned at my old school in Indiana. We used it during football games to cheer for our teams."

"Oh, man," said Rachel. "A ratty old football song? That sounds so dorky!"

"I don't know how to play football," said Barb. "Football is for boys!"

"That's so sexist," said Arielle.

"Let her try." Everyone looked to the doorway. It was Megan standing there with Lizzie. "Maybe she has a good song."

It seemed to Cindy that no one wanted to argue with Megan.

"Go ahead, Cindy," said Megan as she sat down next to Cindy. "Sing!"

Cindy took a deep breath and tried to sing:

"Are we in it? No we're not. We're not in it, we're on top."

She couldn't help it coming out as a whisper. All the girls leaned forward to hear her.

"Come on, louder, Cindy," said Megan. "What are we, deaf or something?"

The other girls laughed. And so did Cindy. She felt confident with Megan there. Cindy took another stab at it.

> *"Are we in it?*
> *No we're not*
> *We're not in it,*
> *We're on top!*

> *"La Dee Dah,*
> *Pink Ladies are the best!*
> *La Dee Dah,*
> *We're better than the rest!*
> *La Dee Dah,*
> *We're gonna wipe you out!*
> *La Dee Dah, La Dee Dah, La Dee Dah.*

> *H-O-T*
> *P-I-N-K*
> *We're hot pink*
> *And that's okay!*

"La Dee Dah,
Pink Ladies are the best!
La Dee Dah,
We're better than the rest!
La Dee Dah,
We're gonna wipe you out!
La Dee Dah, La Dee Dah, La Dee Dah."

By the time Cindy had reached the second verse, Megan started clapping in rhythm. Lizzie joined Megan, and then the other girls followed Lizzie. By the end of the song, the entire cabin was clapping in unison. Cindy was amazed.

"That's a great song!" said Megan.

"Not bad," said Wendy.

"I think it's sexist," said Arielle.

"Zip it, Arielle," said everyone in unison as they rolled their eyes.

Now all the girls started talking at once. Cindy grew excited to think she had started this wave of enthusiasm. Just then Megan stomped her feet. They all quieted down.

"And I have an idea to make it even better!" said Megan. "Gather round and I'll tell you the plan," she said. The girls made an informal huddle. Cindy felt better now that Megan was back on her side.

The next morning, after breakfast, Ruthie and the other counselors gathered around the fireplace in the Meet Hall to start the camp song countdown. Ruthie blew her whistle to quiet down the campers.

"Well, we hope you have your camp songs ready," she said as she looked at Cindy's and the Hot Pink Ladies' table and winked. "This is not a competition. No song is better than another."

A boy in the back of the room groaned, and some of the kids giggled.

"The purpose is to inspire spirit for your cabin, for the camp. A song can be the way you cheer your teammates during a swim class. Or you can use your song to march in time during a hike. Or even to scare away the bears!" said Ruthie.

Everyone in the Meet Hall laughed.

"Are you ready?" asked Ruthie as she held the whistle to her mouth.

"Ready!" yelled back the Meet Hall in unison.

"Let the singing begin!" said Ruthie, and she blew her whistle.

The "Boys in Blue" in Cabin 1 had a song that went something like "Give me an O! Give me a Z! Give me an A! Give me an N! Give me an A! Give me an M! What's that spell?" Everyone in the Meet Hall responded, "Ozanam!"

"See, I told you," said Barb as she leaned over to Cindy. "Football!"

A girl in the Pollywogs Cabin played a guitar that she brought, and her cabin mates sang a song that they wrote to the tune of "Frère Jacques."

The Hot Pink Ladies all looked at one another and nodded.

"Not bad," said Rachel.

And another group of boys called the Jackrabbits took their baseball caps, turned them backward, and sang a cabin song as if they were rap singers.

"I like the cute guy with the black hair," said Barb.

"Shhh, he might hear you," warned Wendy.

"Good," said Barb as she fluffed up her hair.

After each song, the campers in the Meet Hall clapped and whistled. Ruthie was right: The cabin songs were a great icebreaker. Camp spirit was everywhere.

Finally it was the Hot Pink Cabin's turn. Cindy suddenly felt very nervous. What if the other kids laughed at them? What if her bunkmates blamed her? The girls all looked at one another and nodded. They didn't seem to be worried.

"One, two, three," yelled the girls.

They began to clap. CLAP! CLAP! Rachel stood up and clapped her hands over her head as if to get everyone in the Meet Hall to join in. Then Arielle, Barb, Jessie, and even Wendy stood up and clapped their hands. Soon the whole Meet Hall clapped. Even the counselors started to clap. Then the girls started their song.

• • •

"Are we in it? No we're not . . ."

But what made everyone scream out and shout, and what brought a huge grin to Ruthie's face, was that not only did the girls sing their song, but Megan and Lizzie signed it. The kids in the Meet Hall had never seen signing like this before.

"H-O-T P-I-N-K, We're Hot Pink and that's okay!"

Megan and Lizzie finger spelled and signed while the rest of the girls sang.

After a moment, Cindy started signing, too, and surprised herself. In no time, she was able to keep up with Megan and Lizzie. By the time the Hot Pink Cabin got to the end of the song, the whole Meet Hall was on its feet cheering. And, most important, Cindy wasn't the least bit nervous anymore.

Someone in the audience screamed out, "Give me an O!"

The Meet Hall shouted back, "O," while

Megan and Lizzie and Cindy spelled the letter "O" with their hands.

"Give me a 'Z,'" yelled someone else.

This continued back and forth until they spelled out "Ozanam." The Meet Hall cheered again, this time even more loudly.

Ruthie had to blow her whistle to quiet down the Meet Hall. "Camp activities start in five minutes, so clear the Meet Hall so we can get ready," she said. She turned to Cindy and Megan and signed, "You rule!"

Even Cindy understood what Ruthie was signing.

When it was all over, Cindy and the other Hot Pink Ladies gathered together for one big group hug. For the first time in two days, Cindy felt camp was turning out to be fun.

"I guess it wasn't so sexist, after all," said Arielle.

"Zip it, Arielle!" said the rest of the girls as they all laughed.

CHAPTER 13

~

mum's the word

MEGAN AND CINDY SETTLED INTO THE DAILY
routine of camp fun. It was all about hiking
and swimming and horseback riding and
crafts. It also turned out that Megan and
Lizzie became quite popular. After the cabin
song the week before, kids at the camp
begged the counselors for lessons in sign language. Ruthie asked Megan and Lizzie to
take turns holding informal sign lesson circles,
where anyone could drop in and learn a sign
or two.

Megan noticed that Cindy wanted to get
into the act as well by teaching a little sign,
but Megan always made it a point of telling

Cindy that she'd be better off just watching her and Lizzie teach.

"Your signs just aren't good enough!" she said to Cindy one day when Barb asked Cindy how to sign "good morning." It was true. Cindy signed "good morning" so awkwardly that Barb ended up saying, "Thank you, afternoon."

"You should leave the signing to us!" said Megan. With that, she grabbed Lizzie's hand and went running off to the Meet Hall.

One morning a sign on the bulletin board at the Meet Hall announced that it would be "Backward Day." Everyone was to try to walk backward, talk backward, and even wear their clothes backward. Megan, Cindy, and Lizzie did their best that day to be as backward as possible. Megan had all the Hot Pink Cabin Girls wear their clothes inside out and backward.

"It's backward, backward!" Megan said proudly.

Megan saw that Cindy had the hardest time walking since she had put her shoes on the wrong feet. And Lizzie tried to sign backward and made herself almost impossible to understand.

The next day, Megan, Cindy, and Lizzie were relaxing at the lake, dangling their feet in the cool water.

"There should be a quiet day, just like it is down at the lake here, where no one could say anything," Cindy said. "It's could be like Backward Day but without any noise. Of course we'd still be able to talk because we could sign."

"Yeah!" said Lizzie. "Only the three of us could understand one another!"

"It'd be our secret language," said Megan.

"My dad would always say, 'Mum's the word'!" said Cindy.

"What's that mean?" asked Lizzie.

"You know, when you have a secret, you say 'Mum's the word'! It means 'Keep it quiet,'" said Cindy. "We could call it 'Mum's Day.'"

Megan kicked her feet and splashed water on Lizzie and Cindy. "What a perfect idea!"

she shrieked. "Mum's Day! I've got to tell Ruthie!" She scrambled to put on her sandals, then ran to the Meet Hall to find Ruthie.

Megan reported back to the other girls that after a talk with the camp director, Ruthie and the other counselors decided that the next day would be Mum's Day. Everyone in camp, from the counselors to the campers, had to spend the entire day not saying a word. If anyone wanted to say anything, they had to use pantomime or gestures. Not even writing was allowed. Anyone caught saying a word had to drop a nickel into a great big jar situated on the old tree stump next to the flagpole outside of the Meet Hall.

"But what if I see an alligator in the lake and I have to scream out for someone to help me?" asked Arielle that night in the cabin before lights-out.

Megan made the sign for "alligator" by opening and closing the palms of her hands like the jaws of a gator. She added a little snarl for good measure. Arielle shrieked, and the other Hot Pink Ladies laughed.

"Lights out and good night!" said Ruthie as she poked her head in the cabin.

"Good night," said the girls in unison.

The next morning, the camp woke up as usual at 7:00 A.M. Megan got Cindy and Lizzie to hurry up and get dressed. Then all three raced over to the Meet Hall. When they got there, Megan told Cindy and Lizzie she couldn't believe her eyes. At breakfast were row after row of tables with kids miming, gesturing. No one was making a sound! It was like something out of a silent movie. One table was playing a game of charades, but no one could talk back to see if they had the right word or not. Another table used finger spelling they'd learned from Megan and Lizzie to spell out entire sentences to one another. And another table just sat there making funny faces at one another!

"It looks like the United Nations of Sign Language!" signed Lizzie to Megan.

By midday, Megan, Lizzie, and even Cindy were being swamped with requests for last-minute sign and finger-spelling lessons. Boys and girls were lining up in front of the giant jar, having to pay a nickel for each time they spoke. The only ones who still had their nickels were Cindy, Megan, and Lizzie. They never said a word.

At the end of the day, after dinner, Ruthie announced that Mum's Day had been an unqualified success. "Just to let you know, your nickels will be donated to a worthwhile charity. Today we made over forty dollars!" she said.

Ruthie was pleased to see the entire room nod their heads.

"Lastly, I think we should thank Megan for her wonderful idea," said Ruthie.

Instead of clapping, everyone took their cues from Megan, who raised her hands and wiggled them back and forth so everyone could "see" their applause.

"This is how you applaud, sign-language style," said Ruthie as she interpreted for Megan. She demonstrated the "applause" for the Meet Hall.

Suddenly the room was transformed into a

sea of wiggling hands and everyone was
"applauding." Megan looked over at Cindy,
but she wasn't "applauding." Instead, she sat
with her arms folded across her chest, and it
looked like she was angry at something.

"Now if you could all just remember the
lesson in silence you learned today so that
Sunday morning when I want to sleep in an
extra fifteen minutes, you'll all be quiet!"
joked Ruthie. "Oh . . . and one more thing.
You can all talk now! Mum's Day is over!"

The room erupted into a cheer, followed by
a cacophony of laughing and screaming.
Megan could see how everyone was excited
to be able to talk again. It looked like they all
had a lot to say!

"Wasn't that great?" said Megan back at the
cabin as she slipped into her purple pajamas.

The other girls in the Hot Pink Cabin agreed.

"It was, like, awesome!" said Barb.

"I'm going to make my mom and dad do it
back home so I don't have to listen to my stupid sister!" said Rachel.

"That was the best idea you ever had," said

Jessie to Megan.

"I was the one who came up with the idea, not Megan," said Cindy.

Because Cindy's head was bowed down, Megan wasn't sure what she had said. "What did you say?" said Megan.

Cindy looked up. "I said it was my idea, but you took all the credit."

"It was all of us; me, you, and Lizzie," said Megan.

"We all talked about it, but I said it first," said Cindy.

"Was it really her idea?" asked Rachel.

"She wouldn't even have learned sign language in the first place if it weren't for me," said Megan. "She signs because of me and Lizzie!"

Megan saw all the girls make an "OOOOOOOO!" face. They sat up in their bunks. What was the big deal? Did they think there was going to be a fight?

Lizzie tapped Megan on the shoulder and asked her to interpret to Cindy for her. Megan was glad to. She was expecting Lizzie to join her side in the argument.

"I think we're even. We taught you sign, and you gave us the idea for Mum's Day." Megan said the words for Lizzie before she realized what she was saying.

"Thank you for the idea," signed Lizzie. Megan stopped interpreting for her.

"What did she say? What did she say?" said the Hot Pink Girls.

"Tell her!" signed Lizzie to Megan.

"She said . . . thank you," said Megan reluctantly.

Lizzie nudged Megan, as if to say, "Shouldn't you say something?"

Megan had to admit it: Lizzie was right. "Okay, Cindy . . . it was your idea," she said. "But don't forget who taught you sign language in the first place!" And with that she rolled over and pulled her blanket up.

After lights-out, the other girls soon drifted off to sleep, but Megan lay awake thinking. Sometimes she had a lot of fun with Cindy, but sometimes Cindy could make her so mad. Was that all part of having a best friend forever? She tossed and turned into the night.

~

a scary story and scarier storm

"WHO WANTS TO HEAR A SCARY STORY?" called out Mr. Tucker. Cindy quickly learned that Rick Tucker was everyone's favorite counselor at Ozanam. Like everybody else, she loved his grand gestures and tie-dyed clothes. He was spontaneous, unpredictable and, most of all, fun! Even with his floppy mustache, and shiny bald head that he tried to cover with hair from the back of his head, she thought he was the coolest person at camp—next to Ruthie, that is.

It was Sunday night at the big pit fire. This was Cindy's favorite night. It gave everyone a chance to gather together, make some gooey

smores, and catch up on the week's events, and
of course hear one of Mr. Tucker's scary stories. But this particular Sunday was special
because it was the last Sunday at camp.

"Can you believe camp is almost over?"
Cindy asked as she squeezed down next to
Megan. Megan smiled at her but continued to
sign to Lizzie. Ever since Mum's Day, Cindy
noticed that Megan and Lizzie had spent
more and more time together. It used to be
the three of them wandering off to the camp
activities, but lately Megan would take off
with Lizzie and not even bother waiting for
Cindy. Whenever she would bring it up,
Megan would say, "Don't be such a baby."

"Don't forget to write your address down
in my journal," said Barb.

Well, at least I made one friend, Cindy
thought. Then she noticed Barb was saying
the same thing to everyone else. Cindy sighed.

"I said, who wants to hear a scary story?"
Mr. Tucker called out again. This time all the
kids hooted and whistled. "Good, 'cause I've
got one. A story so scary, it will make your hair

stand up straight," said Mr. Tucker as he made a grand sweeping gesture with his pudgy hand. Then he paused for effect. All at once he threw back his comb-over to show off his bald head. All the kids howled with laughter.

"I hadn't told you this story before because it really happened," he went on. Cindy saw some of the campers roll their eyes. Obviously they didn't believe him. "It was a long, long time ago, and it happened right across the lake at Camp Walkeygone."

Jessie raised her hand, "Excuse me, there is no Camp Walkeygone across the lake."

"You're right," said Mr. Tucker. "Now there isn't, but there was. . . ."

All the kids exclaimed, "Oooooo." They huddled closer together. Cindy wanted to hold Megan's hand, but she thought she'd better not. How could she sign, then?

"This particular summer, so many summers ago, Camp Walkeygone was opening for its very first season. But what the campers didn't know was that the camp was built on sacred Native American burial grounds." Some of the kids groaned. They had heard stories about sacred Indian burial grounds.

"Of course, they had permission to build from the tribe," Mr. Tucker was quick to add. The kids laughed. "But they didn't have permission from Hagatha, the witch of the woods. You see, the camp was built where Hagatha grew her garden of special witch herbs. And now, without a garden, Hagatha got very mad. And the one thing you don't want to do is make a witch mad."

A few dark storm clouds rolled in over the lake. A cold wind swept through the trees. Cindy pulled her sweater tightly around her.

"Now I'm sure when I say 'witch,' you're thinking of a withered old woman, hunched over with a wrinkled face." Mr. Tucker hunched over himself and impersonated a witch. The kids laughed. "But that's not Hagatha. She was close to seven feet tall, and with her wild, unwashed hair she was close to nine feet tall. With long, bony fingers that had nails sharpened to a point. Fiery red demon eyes, and her teeth . . ." Mr. Tucker paused and shuddered at the memory. "Well, just do yourself a favor and don't get near her teeth. Hagatha lived in a cave deep in the woods and would only come out at night and then only when the moon was full.

"That first month at Camp Walkeygone was going great. Everybody was playing and having fun. And then came the full moon. The first night of the full moon there was a terrible storm. Rain and thunder and lightning . . ." Cindy looked over at Megan. She was signing the story for Lizzie's benefit, and Cindy could pick out the signs she knew for rain and thunder and lightning.

"The next morning, when the campers came out of their cabins, they discovered all the horses and dogs and cats were gone. They thought they must have gotten scared in the storm and run away. That was until they started to find these twigs tied in the middle to form an X. See, Hagatha didn't know how to read or write, and the only mark she made was an 'X.'"

Cindy looked around the fire circle at all

the campers. Nobody was laughing now. It seemed as though Mr. Tucker's scary story was working. "The second night of the full moon there was no storm but something far scarier. Right around midnight, the witching hour, the woods were full of weird noises. Horrible howls . . ."

And, right on cue, off in the woods, came a horrible howl. Barb screamed. That set off more screams. Cindy didn't take her eyes off Mr. Tucker. He acted like he didn't hear anything. He was too involved with his story. "And there were gut-wrenching screeches . . ."

From the other side of the camp came a gut-wrenching screech. The kids jumped and laughed nervously. Cindy saw Megan and Lizzie look around, not being able to understand what everyone was reacting to. She signed to them about the noises in the woods. "Oh, please," said Megan as she rolled her eyes.

"The next day everyone's nerves were on edge, and they all vowed not to fall asleep because they knew if they fell asleep and let down their guard, Hagatha could steal them away. So the whole camp stayed up except ... one cabin with a group of nine-year-old girls." When he said that, he looked right at the Hot Pink Ladies. Thunder rumbled in the distance. Barb screamed again and buried her head in Cindy's shoulder.

"The next morning, all those girls were gone, and left on their pillows were two twigs tied together like this!" With that, Mr. Tucker held up an "X" made out of twigs. Everyone screamed. Even Cindy.

All at once a huge, shadowy figure leaped into the middle of the circle. It was over seven feet tall and shrouded in black. A cloaked hood covered its face. Two long arms waved menacingly around the group. All the kids screamed and yelled, clutching one another. Megan hollered, jumped to her feet, and ran behind a tree.

Just then all the counselors burst out laughing. The shrouded figure collapsed to the ground. It was really a large puppet being controlled by Ruthie, who was underneath

the black cloak. When Cindy saw this, she let
out a sigh of relief. She wasn't alone.

Everyone began talking at once about the
good scare. Cindy looked behind her as
Megan slowly crept back to the circle. She
tried to join in the laughter.

"Gee, Megan, I never saw anybody run so
fast!" said Cindy.

"And I thought I was scared," said Arielle.

"Megan, you totally freaked out," Wendy
chimed in.

"I wasn't scared," Megan said defiantly. "I
just wanted to get a better look. I knew it was
a fake all along."

"Yeah, right," said Rachel.

All the girls were laughing and having a
good time, but Cindy recognized that look on
Megan's face. She was starting to fume. "Hey,
we're only kidding," she signed to Megan.

Megan didn't respond. Instead, she just
folded her arms in front of her. Just then it
started to rain. All the campers scrambled to
get back to their cabins.

Inside the Hot Pink Cabin, the girls were

talking all at once and drying themselves from the rain. Thunder and lightning continued to crack outside. With each bolt, the girls screamed and laughed. All at once the lights went out.

"Oh, no," cried Arielle.

"It's just a blackout," said Rachel. "Look!" The girls gathered around the window and they could see all the lights in the camp were out. They each hurried to get their flashlights. The thunder was still cracking loudly, and lightning flashed.

Cindy made her way over to Megan's bunk. "Are you okay?" she asked, shining her flashlight in Megan's face.

"I will be if you get that light out of my eyes," Megan shot back.

Just then the door of the cabin slammed open.

"It's Hagatha," Rachel called out. The girls screamed. Megan ducked under her covers. But it was only Ruthie standing at the door in her rain slicker.

"Very funny," Ruthie said. "Everybody here

and safe? Good. Settle in and don't go outside."

"And we're not going to sleep, either!"
Jessie said. All the girls agreed.

"Suit yourself," Ruthie said with a smile as
she head back out into the rain.

Cindy stood up to look out the window,
but she was really checking on Megan. Lizzie
crossed over to Megan's bunk and pulled
down her blanket. "Why are you hiding?" she
signed. "It's only a thunderstorm."

"I'm not hiding!" Megan said angrily. "Why
doesn't everybody just go and scare themselves?" Cindy saw that nobody was paying
attention to Megan's outburst. They seemed to
be too caught up in the storm and the story of
Hagatha.

"What if we have to go to the bathroom in
the middle of the night?" Arielle asked with a
worried look.

"Then go," Rachel said.

"Just watch out for Hagatha," Lizzie signed.
When Megan didn't interpret for her, Cindy
jumped in.

As the girls settled into their bunks, Cindy wandered over to Megan. She was sitting on her bunk reading her comics and not joining in on any of the laughter or fun. "What's the matter?" Cindy asked.

"Nothing," Megan answered without looking up.

"You're not upset, 'cause we were teasing you, are you?"

"For your information, I'm not upset," Megan said.

"It's okay to be scared. We all were. It's kind of fun. Like a roller-coaster ride."

"I was not scared!"

"Okay," Cindy said. She knew better than to push her. Before she turned away to go into her own bunk, Cindy noticed for the first time that Megan had her old purple blanket under her pillow. She must really be upset.

Cindy climbed into her bunk. The girls stayed up chattering as the storm drifted away. Soon they all fell off to sleep, still clutching their flashlights.

Sometime late in the night, Cindy woke up

with a start. The thunder and rain had stopped. Everything was quiet outside. She'd had a bad dream about being lost in the woods. She wanted to share her nightmare with someone, and when she glanced over at Megan's bed, she saw that Megan was gone. All that was on her pillow were two twigs tied in an "X."

CHAPTER 15

~

megan is lost

I'LL SHOW THEM WHO'S SCARED, MEGAN thought as she left the cabin in the middle of the night. Right after the other girls had drifted off to sleep, Megan came up with the brilliant idea to give the Hot Pink Ladies a real scare. She tiptoed out of the cabin and found two twigs. She hurriedly tied them into the "X," just like the ones in Mr. Tucker's Hagatha story. Her plan was to sneak out behind the cabin and let them discover her missing. She only wished she could see the looks on their faces when they found the "X" twigs.

The storm had passed, and everything was

wet. The air was filled with the smell of damp leaves. Even though it was still dark out, Megan wasn't worried. That only proved she wasn't scared. She didn't even feel the need to take her purple blanket with her. Megan wondered what the lake would look like under the full moon. She decided to walk down the trail that led to the water. It cut through the forest and was very twisting and turning. Besides, it wasn't that far, and she liked the smell of the wet cedar chips on the trail.

When Megan rounded a corner, she came upon a tree that had fallen across the path. She could either climb over, or go around it. Megan stopped and leaned against the tree trunk to consider her options. She took out a piece of grape bubble gum and unwrapped it. Just as she plopped it into her mouth, a deer came out of the woods and stood on the path not twenty feet from where Megan was resting.

Megan froze. The deer turned its head and looked straight at Megan but didn't move. Megan held her breath. Just then a baby deer came out of the woods and nuzzled up to its mother. The baby deer looked toward Megan. Megan smiled, and the two deer wandered off into the woods.

Megan hurried back up the path and turned into the woods after the deer. They were walking slowly, and she made sure she kept her distance. She imagined she was a great Native American tracker, following the deer back to their home. The deer were moving a little more swiftly, so Megan had to run a bit to catch up.

Suddenly they stopped in their tracks. So did Megan. The mother deer raised up her head and sniffed the air. Megan did the same. All she could smell were the wet leaves and her grape bubble gum. Was that what the deer was sniffing? She took out the gum and dropped it to the ground. With that, the deer took off running. Megan laughed, and without thinking she ran after them. But they were too fast. Soon they were gone out of sight. Megan stopped to catch her breath. She looked around her. Something didn't feel right. Then she realized she didn't recognize this part of the woods.

Megan looked up and saw a few stars poking through the overhang of the trees. She turned around to head back the way she had come, but now she couldn't remember the way. She headed off in a direction she thought was right but ended up in a deep thicket of bushes. This couldn't have been the way. So she turned around and went in another direction. Now she was really confused.

Megan stopped and sat down, leaning against a tree. She looked around her. The trees seemed to close in around her. They couldn't have moved, could they? She was getting scared and she wished she had brought her purple blanket. She didn't know what to do. *Maybe when the sun comes up I'll know where I am,* she thought. Until then, she would wait. But these trees . . . were they reaching out for her? Megan pulled the hood up from her jacket and yanked it down over her eyes. She sat like that shivering in the cold.

CHAPTER 16

~

the search

CINDY WAS REALLY SCARED. SHE WASN'T sure what she should do when she found the twig "X" on Megan's pillow. Should she wake the others? Go find Ruthie? She didn't know. Maybe Megan was playing a trick? Or maybe there really was a Hagatha in the woods.

Summoning up her courage, she stepped outside of the cabin. The sky was slowly turning from the dark of night to the red of morning. Everything was quiet and still. Even the birds weren't chirping.

"Megan?" she called out. Then she realized how silly that was. Megan couldn't hear her. Now she really got worried. She walked around the cabin, but Megan wasn't hiding there. Cindy knew she had to tell the other girls. She went back into the cabin and flipped on the lights.

"You guys . . . ," she said, standing in the middle of the room. None of the girls woke up. "Hey!" she said loudly. "Wake up! Come on! Wake up!" Cindy surprised herself for being forceful. She went around shaking everybody up from the beds.

"What's going on?" Wendy asked as she rubbed her eyes.

"Leave me alone," Rachel snapped.

Cindy tapped on Lizzie's shoulder and signed for her to wake up. She continued to sign for her benefit while she told the girls what was happening.

"Megan's gone, and I found this on her pillow." Cindy held up the twig "X."

The girls all groaned.

"Oh, like that's for real," Barb said.

"Give me a break," Rachel said, and pulled her covers up over her head to keep out the light.

"I'm serious," Cindy said. "She's gone. I've been up and walked around outside. She's not anywhere."

"So what do you want us to do?" Jessie asked.

"I think we should go look for her," Cindy said.

"If this is some kind of joke, you're going to get it," Rachel said.

Arielle came over to Cindy. "I think we should tell Ruthie."

"Let's wait until we look around first," Cindy said. "Everybody grab your flashlights and come with me. Hurry!"

The girls pulled on their shoes and wrapped up in their sweat jackets. They got their flashlights and joined Cindy outside the cabin.

"Okay, I think we should split up," Cindy said. "Barb and Rachel, you go check out around the other cabins and the Meet Hall. Jessie and Wendy, check out the stables and the ball fields. I'll go down the trails by the lake. Lizzie, you stay here in case she comes back. If she does, ring the meet bell and we'll all come back. And remember, she's not going to be able to hear you."

"So how are we going to find her?" Barb asked.

"Just look!" Cindy said, and she took off toward the lake with Arielle.

Walking down the trail, Cindy and Arielle shined their flashlights into the woods.

"Megan!" Arielle called out. "Oops, I forgot." They walked a little while longer until they came to the fallen tree. Arielle screamed when she saw it.

"What's the matter?" Cindy asked.

"What if Megan is underneath the tree?" she said.

"Give me a break," Cindy said. But what if she was? In *The Wizard of Oz*, Dorothy's house had fallen on the wicked witch. The girls slowly walked to the tree. Cindy sighed with relief when she didn't see anything under the tree. But there on the ground she saw a piece of paper and bent down and picked it up.

"What's that?"

"It's one of Megan's gum wrappers," Cindy said. "She was probably here."

"She could have dropped that anytime," Arielle said.

Cindy passed the wrapper from one hand to the other. Then it came to her. "No! This is dry. If she had dropped it before the storm, it would be wet. She was here! We've got to go into the woods."

"I'm not going in those woods," Arielle said, pulling away from Cindy. "Hagatha is in there."

"Then run and get everybody else. Tell them to come down to the trail and spread out from here." Before Arielle had a chance to answer, Cindy headed off into the woods.

The sun was higher now, and the woods started to come alive. She flipped off her flashlight and kept on walking. Birds began chirping. They made it seem like everything was going to be okay. But wherever Megan was, she couldn't hear the birds. For the first time, Cindy really understood what it was like not to hear even the simplest of sounds.

After a few minutes of making her way through the woods, Cindy wasn't sure where she was. She couldn't see the trail behind her, and she couldn't see the lake. She stopped to listen. No sounds except for the birds. She kept walking. Another twenty feet or so she stopped again to listen. Cindy thought she heard something rustle in the branches just up ahead. Now here were sounds that scared her. Maybe if she were deaf like Megan she wouldn't be so scared right now. Then she heard something else. Something strange that didn't belong in the woods. Was that crying?

"Megan?" Cindy made her way toward the noise. She stopped again and heard it stronger. It was someone crying! Excited, she ran toward the noise, not even seeing the tree branch on the ground until it was too late. She tripped and went sprawling on the ground.

CHAPTER 17

~

lost and found

MEGAN STAYED AGAINST THE TREE WITH HER hood pulled over her head for a long time. She didn't know how long. But when she finally took the hood off, it was starting to get light out. That made Megan feel a little bit better. She stood up and looked around. Now the woods looked more like woods and not some scary place where a witch might live. She turned around to see if anything looked familiar. Nothing did. Megan started walking.

She wasn't sure where she was heading, but thought the woods had to end somewhere. The damp woods smells were much stronger out here. A squirrel raced in front of her and scampered up the tree. Was he lost, too? At least he could climb up high and have a look around.

After walking for a few minutes, Megan didn't see any break in the woods. She stopped and decided to head in another direction. That wasn't any help. Now she was getting frustrated.

"Hello!" Megan hollered out. But of course she couldn't hear if anyone answered her. She kicked the dirt. She picked up a stick and smashed it against the tree. That felt good, but it didn't do any good. She leaned back against a tree and started to cry.

"Stupid deer!" she said as she broke the stick in half. Megan slid down the tree trunk and plopped on the ground. What were Mom and Dad and Matt doing right now? What if they never saw her again? She started to put her thumb in her mouth but stopped. "I don't want to be a baby," she said to herself.

All at once something came crashing through the woods and fell down right in front of her. Megan looked up, frightened, and saw it was Cindy. She had tripped. Cindy looked up and saw her friend and hollered out, "Megan!"

"Cindy!" The two girls jumped up and hugged each other.

"You skinned your knee," Megan pointed out to her.

"What are you doing here?" Cindy asked.

"I got lost," Megan said.

"Why?"

"I was going to play a joke on everybody to prove I wasn't scared, and then I came down the trail and saw two deer. I followed them into the woods and then got lost," Megan explained.

"Serves you right," Cindy said.

"I'm sorry," Megan said. She hugged Cindy again. "I'm just glad you found me."

"Well . . . ," Cindy said, worried.

"What's the matter?"

"I'm kind of lost, too," Cindy said.

"What?" Megan couldn't believe it. Just when she thought she was saved.

"But it's okay. We can find a way out of

here," Cindy said. She took Megan by the hand, and they started walking together.

"HELLO! WE'RE HERE! WE'RE HERE!" Cindy started calling out. Megan could see what she was doing and started hollering as well. They kept walking and hollering. After several minutes, Cindy stopped.

"What?" Megan asked.

"I hear someone," Cindy said. "OVER HERE!" she called out. Cindy took Megan by the hand and dragged her off in another direction. Before they knew it, they saw Ruthie and one of the other counselors coming through the woods toward them.

"Hey!" Megan said when she saw them. The two girls ran up to the counselors.

"Are you okay?" Ruthie asked as she knelt down, checking out each of the girls.

"I'm okay, but Cindy scraped her knee when she tripped," Megan pointed out.

"Well, we can take care of that," Ruthie said. "Let's get back to camp."

"But aren't you lost, too?" Megan asked. Ruthie smiled and took the girls by the hand.

After walking a little bit, they came right out onto the trail; apparently Ruthie knew exactly where they were. They made it up to the camp, where it looked like everyone was waiting for them. When the campers saw them coming off the trail, they all let out a cheer.

"Safe and sound," Ruthie declared.

The Hot Pink girls gathered around Megan and Cindy. They were all talking at once, telling them how worried they had been.

"Good thing Cindy made us go look for you," Rachel said.

"Yeah, you could have been out there forever," Arielle said. "Cindy is a real hero."

"I would have found my way out sooner or later," Megan said, defending herself.

"Not without Cindy!" Barb was quick to add. Megan saw all the girls pat Cindy on the back and congratulate her. But she was the one who'd spent the night in the scary woods. Didn't that deserve congratulations?

Ruthie came up to them. "Megan, I hoped you learned your lesson about wandering off alone?" she said.

"I guess so." She kicked some dirt at her feet.

"Come on, Cindy, let's clean up that scrape," Ruthie said, taking Cindy off by the hand. The other girls followed. Megan stayed behind. Lizzie came up and tapped her on the shoulder.

"I'm glad you're okay," she signed.

"Thanks," Megan signed back.

"You know, we really shouldn't go off like that," Lizzie continued.

"What do you mean 'we'?" Megan asked.

"You know, because we're deaf. It's a good thing you have a friend like Cindy to help you," Lizzie signed.

This didn't make Megan feel good; it only made her more angry.

CHAPTER 18

~

good-bye, camp ozanam

AFTER THE BIG EXCITEMENT OF MEGAN
getting lost, things quickly got back to normal
fast. Cindy and her bunkmates began to pack
up all their belongings. The session was almost
over.

The night before, at the final sing-along
down at the lake, the Hot Pink Ladies had
promised they wouldn't cry. It almost seemed
they would keep their promise when they
sang, along with Cindy, Megan, and Lizzie
signing the words. But when the shadows of
their hands moving in rhythm with their song
flickered on the trees as the campfire popped
and crackled, everyone put their arms around

one another's shoulders and swayed back and forth as they sang. Cindy could see some of them crying and heard their sniffles.

"One more time!" yelled Ruthie as the last cabin finished their song.

The kids hollered and whooped. Camp was finally over.

The next morning as the girls of the Hot Pink Cabin stood around waiting to board the buses, it was easy for Cindy to see that most of them wished they were still in their beds.

"When I get home, I'm going to sleep for hours," said Rachel.

"I'm going to sleep for days," said Jessie.

"Months!" said Barb.

Ruthie blew her whistle and began to read off the list of campers to make sure everyone was ready.

Cindy and Lizzie were hugging each other when Ruthie tapped Lizzie on the shoulder to tell her that it was time to board her bus.

"Don't forget to send me e-mail!" said Lizzie as she hugged Cindy one last time.

"You and Megan should definitely come to visit. You're only an hour away!" said Lizzie.

"Sure!" said Cindy. "I promise." Cindy didn't tell Lizzie that she and Megan had hardly spoken to each other since the whole woods incident. Cindy had tried to talk to Megan but had gotten only one-word answers. She wondered if Megan was embarrassed about getting caught in trying to pull off a joke. She didn't like it when Megan got like this.

"Can we say one more good-bye to everybody before we go?" Lizzie asked Ruthie.

"Hurry up!" said Ruthie. "You have five minutes."

Lizzie grabbed Cindy by the hand and dragged Cindy into the crowd of campers loading up the buses. As they were hugging everyone good-bye, Cindy saw Megan step over to Ruthie. Because they were signing to each other, Cindy could understand their conversation. She knew it was wrong to "eavesdrop," but she wanted to know what was wrong with Megan.

"I bet you and Cindy are excited to be

going home," said Ruthie. "School is just around the corner."

"Whatever," said Megan.

"Well, I've got to say, I'm glad you guys came to Ozanam. I got to practice my signs. Now I can say the things I always wanted to say to my sister."

Cindy could see Megan shuffling back and forth on her feet. She knew Megan was getting a little impatient waiting to get on the bus.

"Don't you want to know what I want to say?" said Ruthie.

"Uh, sure," said Megan.

"I was thinking the thing that I always wanted to say was I'm sorry," said Ruthie.

Cindy saw the puzzled look on Megan.

"Sorry? What are you sorry for?" said Megan.

"Lots of things. But mostly for not listening to her," said Ruthie.

Ruthie stopped signing and just looked at Megan for a moment. Then she went back to her checklist. Cindy caught Megan's eye as she glanced over in her direction. She couldn't tell what she was thinking.

"Hey, there's Megan!" said Lizzie, running back up to Cindy. "Come on!" Once again she dragged Cindy by the hand.

"Thanks so much! I'm going to miss you guys!" said Lizzie, and she gave them both one last hug.

"There's your bus, Lizzie. And your bus is over there," said Ruthie to Megan and Cindy. "Hurry up! You don't want to get left behind and have to spend all winter here."

"No way!" said Megan. She grabbed her bag and ran onto the big bus without waiting for Cindy.

Cindy handed her bags to the bus driver to load. She was the last one to get on the bus. Before she climbed on board, she looked around for one last time at the camp.

The bus was completely full except for one seat on the aisle. She ran to the seat, hoping it was Megan who had saved it for her. She wanted to talk to her on the way home.

But when she got to the seat, she found it

was the cute boy from the Jackrabbit Cabin. She looked around, hoping there was another seat, but in the very back was Megan, sitting next to a girl from the Pollywogs Cabin.

"We can't go until you sit down back there," yelled the bus driver.

Barb, who was sitting across the aisle from Cindy, tugged at her shirt and pointed to the driver. Cindy had no choice but to sit down.

"I'm glad I get to sit next to someone I know," said Barb. "Plus, you're sitting next to that cute guy!" Barb signed this last part to Cindy. They all had gotten quite good at signing.

"Yeah," said Cindy. She tried to get Megan's attention in the back of the bus, but Megan wouldn't look up.

The bus rumbled out of the parking lot and past the sign that said CAMP OZANAM. Everyone turned around and waved one last time.

After fifteen minutes, Cindy fell asleep. She slept the whole trip home. When she woke up, everyone was exiting the bus and Megan was gone. During the entire five-hour trip, she'd never gotten a chance to talk to her.

She told this to her mother in the YMCA parking lot where the bus had dropped off all the campers. But her mother seemed too busy hugging her to pay attention. "You can talk to Megan later," said Grace.

But Cindy was still looking around for Megan. She saw her across the parking lot loading her bag into the back of her family's station wagon. Cindy waved, and Megan looked right at her. But instead of waving back, she just turned around and got into the car.

"Come on, honey," said Grace as she picked up Cindy's bag. "We've got a lot of catching up to do." Cindy had no choice but to get in the car. It was official. Megan wasn't speaking to her.

~

caution: deaf child crossing

MEGAN WAS VERY EXCITED TO SEE HER
mother. She forgot all about being angry with
Cindy. As soon as they got into the car she was
talking a mile a minute about all the excitement of camp and getting lost in the woods
and everything else. When she finally finished
her stories, Megan asked about the family and
Apples as she rolled down the window to
smell the hot summer air. Fresh-cut lawns. She
had missed that smell up in the woods.

"Would you like to stop off at Mrs. Kim's
before we go home?" Lainee asked. Something
was wrong here. It was usually Megan who
always had to beg and plead to go to Mrs.
Kim's for ice cream.

"Can't we just go home? It sounds wierd, but I miss Apples."

Megan noticed her mother's eyes getting all watery.

"What's the matter?" Megan asked.

Lainee took a deep breath and sighed. "Darling, I'm so sorry, but while you were away, we had to put Apples to sleep," said Lainee.

Megan wasn't sure what that meant. Before her mother could say anything else, they pulled into their driveway and Megan hopped out of the car. She expected her brother to pick on her like he always did. But when she saw Matt, he wasn't his usual self. Megan thought he was just being dorky. She asked if Apples was still sleeping. Megan saw Matt look over at Lainee. She was wiping away a tear. Now Megan knew something was wrong.

"Apples isn't sleeping. He died last week," said Matt.

At first, Megan didn't say anything. She just couldn't believe it. "Apples can't be dead," said Megan. "He can't."

Apples had been around her entire life. How could he be gone? Megan searched the house, hoping Apples was just hiding. But he wasn't hiding. In fact, he wasn't there at all. His bowl was gone. His bed was gone. Even his funny smell was gone.

David and Lainee had to sit down and tell Megan that Matt was not lying. Apples had died.

"But Apples was only thirteen years old!" said Megan, crying. Then Megan got a horrible thought. "I'm only ten! Does that mean I'll die, too?"

David hugged Megan as she cried. Then he lifted her chin. "He was thirteen years old in people years, but that's ninety-one years old in dog years. That was very, very old for a dog."

"Older than Grandma Josie?" asked Megan. Grandma Josie was the oldest person Megan knew.

"Much, much older," said David.

Lainee came up to Megan and gently put her arms around her. "It's going to be okay, honey," she said. "I'm sure Apples is up in heaven right now, running around and playing with a whole bunch of other dogs."

Megan liked the thought of that, but she was still upset.

"Why don't you go upstairs and unpack?" Lainee suggested as she wiped away Megan's tears. "Maybe later we'll order a pizza with all your favorite toppings."

As she went up to her room, Megan was remembering everything she could about Apples. How he used to follow her to the front door every morning before she left for school, and how it was Apples who had greeted her every afternoon when she came home. And it was Apples who had sat with her for hours and hours while she'd listened to Billy Joel when everyone else had complained and asked her to turn down the music. Apples was really her first best friend.

And then Megan thought of something else. Something amazing. As upset as she was, she didn't once reach for her old purple blanket or suck her thumb. The last time she'd wanted to have it was in the woods. She

wiped her eyes and went to her backpack.
She unzipped it and pulled out the blanket.
She sniffed it. Apples! Her blanket still smelled
a little like him. She remembered how he had
liked to chew on it and play tug-of-war. She
held the blanket up to her nose for a few minutes more. It wasn't a bad smell after all. She
put it away in her clothes drawer. She didn't
want her mom ever to wash it again. She
never wanted to forget Apples's smell.

A few days later, Megan was at her desk
writing when her mother came into the room
with some clean sheets. "What's this?" she
asked, pointing to a picture of Apples on
Megan's desk.

"It's so I'll always have him around."

"He looks like an old man in this picture,"
said Lainee as she sat down on the bed.

Megan smiled a half-smile.

"I spoke with Cindy's mother yesterday,"
said Lainee.

Megan didn't say anything.

"She said Cindy has been moping around

the house all day," said Lainee. "Guess she misses Apples, too, huh?"

"Yeah, right," said Megan. She didn't feel much like telling her mother what had happened at camp.

Lainee got up from the bed and walked over to Megan's desk. She picked up the picture of Apples and looked at it closely. "He was your first best friend, wasn't he?" said Lainee.

"Yeah," said Megan. "But sometimes I was so mean to him. I didn't always want him in my bed. And sometimes I pushed him away when he tried to lick my face. I wish he were here now. I'd let him lick my face." With that, she put her head in her arms and started to cry a little.

She felt her mother stroking her hair. Megan looked up at Lainee.

"Even when he would follow you everywhere you went and you complained he was such a pest, you knew deep down inside he really loved you," said Lainee. "And you loved him, too, even when you pushed him away."

deaf child crossing

Megan nodded her head and wiped her eyes.

"It's all about being able to forgive and forget," said Lainee.

Megan nodded.

"And it's about saying 'I'm sorry' even though you're still angry. Without that, you can't ever tell your friends that you love them," said Lainee.

"I don't love Cindy!" said Megan.

"Who's talking about Cindy?" said Lainee. She put the picture of Apples back down on Megan's desk. "I was talking about Apples. You know, we should go to Powell's just before school starts to shop for school clothes. Wouldn't you like Cindy to come along?"

"No . . . ," said Megan weakly. "She'd try to help me and tell me what to do. She'll never change."

"Remember how shy and afraid she was when she moved here? And remember how stubborn you were until you learned how to tell her when you needed help?" said Lainee.

"Yeah," said Megan as she straightened the pencils on her desk. "But at camp she tried to be real bossy and take credit for everything," said Megan.

"Well, I don't know all the details, but I know that Cindy is probably the best friend you have. Next to Apples, of course," said Lainee.

"No, she's not," said Megan.

"Stubbornness just runs in the Merrill family, doesn't it?" asked Lainee.

Megan nodded her head. Just then, her father poked his head in the room. "It's here," he said to Lainee.

"What's here?" Megan asked.

"Actually the thing that's here is for you."

Megan thought about another package from Grandma Josie. She jumped up and ran out of the room.

She practically flew down the stairs to the living room, but there was no package or box from Grandma Josie. Matt was standing by the front door and looking out in the street. Megan came up to him. "Where's my present?"

"What present?" he asked.

"Dad said it was here."

"Yeah, but it's not a dopey present," Matt said, and he just pointed outside.

Megan stepped out onto the porch. Down the street, on the corner, she could see a few workmen wearing bright orange vests over their work clothes. They were using shovels to pat the dirt around a new sign that had just been put in. Megan couldn't see what the sign said. She looked back at her house to see Matt and her parents coming out. "What's going on?" she asked.

"Check it out," Matt said, and pointed to the sign.

Now Megan was really curious. She ran to the corner just as the workmen were packing up all their tools. Megan came around to the other side of the sign and looked up. It was a bright yellow diamond with black lettering that said, CAUTION: DEAF CHILD CROSSING. Megan couldn't believe it. This was a sign just for her. Just then, her parents came up to join her.

"Pretty cool," Matt said. Lainee had her

camera and started snapping pictures.

"What's this all about?" Megan asked.

"I talked to the city and got the sign put up. It's about time, wouldn't you say?" her dad said. "Now everyone will slow down and think twice when they drive through the neighborhood."

"All because of me?" Megan asked.

"Of course," Lainee said.

"So it's to help me?"

"Yeah, unless you want to stop every car and tell them you might be running all around and can't hear them," Matt said. "Of course with your motormouth, you'd probably like doing that." She wasn't going to get mad at him for that. This was too exciting. She walked around the sign a couple of times. She touched the pole. It was shiny and new. Not like the other street signs that were rusty.

"I know what," said Lainee. "Why don't I finally keep that romise I made and take you to Mrs. Kim's Ice-cream Shop to celebrate. We can share a Colossus. Or two? Or three? How about that?"

It had been almost a month since she'd had one of her favorite ice-cream dishes from Mrs. Kim's.

"Like we'll ever get to eat any with her," Matt said as he headed back to the house. Megan just wanted to stand out there all afternoon and look at her sign. Her father came up and put his hands on her shoulders.

"It's okay to ask for a little help, Megan," he said. "And the help you get you give it back."

Maybe he was right.

The next day was the first day of school, and Megan was really excited about going. She practically raced out of the house. She wanted to be the first one on the corner, under her sign, waiting for the bus.

And she was. One by one the other kids gathered at the bus stop. They all looked up at the new sign, then at Megan. She was smiling proudly.

Cindy was the last one to come over to the group, and she stood in the back. There's no way she could see the sign from there. Megan wandered over to her.

"Hey."

"Hey, yourself," Cindy said.

"Ready for the big day?" Megan asked, trying to draw her into conversation.

Cindy just shrugged.

"So now you're not talking to me?"

"Hey, you're the one not talking to me," Cindy shot back.

"You can be so stubborn sometimes," Megan said.

Megan could see Cindy's face flush red. All at once she threw down her books and lunged for Megan. She grabbed her hair, hard. Megan instinctively grabbed Cindy's hair back. It was the first time Megan had been in a fight like this.

Out of the corner of her eye, Megan saw the other kids gather around in a circle.

Bobby Michels was calling out, "Fight! Fight!"

"You take that back!" yelled Cindy.

"It's the truth!" said Megan.

"You are so bossy and mean!" said Cindy as she pulled harder on Megan's hair.

Megan yelped, then saw both her mom and Cindy's mom coming through the crowd of school kids.

"Cindy! Megan!" called both mothers. "What are you doing?"

Lainee tugged on Megan and pulled her to her feet. Grace did the same to Cindy.

"I wish we'd never moved here!" said Cindy. The veins in her forehead bulged out, and Megan noticed she was spitting as she spoke. "I'm sick of hanging around a girl who talks funny and has bubble gum in her ears! She's so stupid!" said Cindy.

"Cindy Calicchio, I'm ashamed of you!" said Grace. "Apologize this minute!" Cindy's mother had never seen her daughter so angry in her life.

"She's mean!" said Cindy.

"And I'm stupid!" said Megan.

"And she's bossy," said Cindy.

"Don't forget stubborn!" Megan said. She smiled at Cindy.

"And she's . . ." Cindy stopped. "Huh?"

Megan saw Matt come running over. But

when he saw the fight was over, he threw up his hands. "I always miss the best stuff," he said.

"I'm the loudmouth, always taking credit, and the one who doesn't share," said Megan.

She could tell by the look on Cindy's face that she was completely confused. It looked like everyone who was standing there was confused. That was funny.

Megan took Cindy by the hand and brought her around to the front of the sign. She pointed up.

"What's all this about?" Cindy asked.

"You found me in the woods when I was stupid to run off. It was the bravest thing anyone could do."

"What?" said Cindy.

"Yep!" said Megan. "No matter who you are, sometime you're going to need help."

Cindy's mouth hung open like that cartoon character again.

"I'm very proud of you," said Lainee.

"Mom, don't get all gushy on me in front of everybody."

Grace helped pick up Cindy's books.

"I'll be okay, Mom," said Cindy. "Really."

Grace kissed Cindy good-bye. She then turned to Megan. "Thank you. I think you two are very brave little girls." She walked back home across Morton Street.

"Okay, fight's over!" said Bobby Michels.

Lainee pinched her daughter's cheek and walked back to her house.

Megan and Cindy stood there for what seemed like the longest minute without saying anything.

"You're still wearing the friendship bracelet," said Megan.

"Yeah," said Cindy as she fiddled with it.

"Do you really think I talk funny and wear bubble gum in my ears?" asked Megan.

"Don't you remember I said that the first day we met?" said Cindy as she smiled. "That was a long time ago."

"Like a million years," said Megan.

"Still friends," said Megan, and she held out her index finger.

She waited for a second. Then Cindy held out her finger and grabbed Megan's finger.

She turned their hands over to make the sign for "friend."

Just then the bus pulled up, and the other kids started to pile on. Megan stood looking up at her sign.

"Megan, aren't you coming to school today?" said Mrs. Cruthers, the bus driver. "You're going to be late! Megan? Megan?"

Cindy jumped off the bus and ran over to Megan.

"What are you, deaf or something?" said Cindy.

Megan laughed very hard. Cindy was happy to hear that laugh again.

"Let's go, Hot Pink Lady," said Cindy.

"I'm coming, I'm coming!" said Megan.

Megan and Cindy jumped on the bus and took a seat toward the back.

As the bus drove off, Megan turned to Cindy and finger spelled three letters. "BFF," said Megan. "Best friends forever."